Mask of Nobility

Scandalous Scions Story 4.0

TRACY
COOPER-POSEY

STORIES RULE

EDMONTON • ALBERTA

Praise for

The Scandalous Scions Series

If you are familiar with the previous series, I'am sure you fell in love with the huge family like I did.

She is a go to author for me when I need a fix of historical romance.

Tracy Cooper-Posey takes us into the staid yet surprisingly bawdy Victorian Era where appearance is everything and secrets are held inside the family.

Thanks once again, Tracy Cooper-Posey, for giving us another great story and for giving me back my love of historical romances.

I love historical romances and this one filled all my likes, from a dashing, wonderful hero, a beautiful strong heroine, a love story to sigh over, side characters that are interesting, and funny, and move the story along.

I can't wait for the next in this wonderful new series.

I don't often give books five stars, but I really enjoyed the mystery that puzzled all of the characters in this story.

I found the entire extended family intriguing because they, the women in particular, are very aware and careful of what society will think, yet they often have made choices that are deemed semi- scandalous.

A wonderful story set in the Victorian era of such strict social conventions and yet the main characters are shimmering with latent sexual tension. What a fabulous juxtaposition!

Another great series is starting and it looks like it will be great just like all the other series by this author.

Wow, as soon as I started Tracy Cooper Posey's first book in her new spin off I was hooked.

The Great Family

Elisa and Vaughn Wardell

Marquess of Fairleigh, Viscount Rothmere

1825 Raymond, Viscount Marblethorpe (stepson)
1839 William Vaughn Wardell
1839 John (Jack) Gladwin Lochlann Mayes (fostered in 1846)
1842 Sarah Louise Wardell (D)
1843 Peter Lovell Wardell
1844 Gwendolyn (Jenny) Violet Moore Wardell (adopted in 1848)
1844 Patricia Sharla Victoria Mayes (fostered in 1846)
1849 Blanche Brigitte Colombe Bonnay (adopted in 1851)
1853 Emma Jane Wardell (adopted at birth)

Natasha and Seth Williams

Earl of Innesford, Baron Harrow (Ire.)

1839 Lillian Mary Harrow
1840 Richard Cian Seth Williams
1841 Neil Vaughn Williams
1843 Daniel Rhys Williams
1846 Bridget Bronte Williams & Mairin May Williams
1849 Annalies Grace Williams

Annalies and Rhys Davies

Princess Annalies Benedickta of Saxe-Weiden, of the royal house Saxe-Coburg-Weiden, Formerly of the Principality of Saxe-Weiden.

1835 Benjamin Hedley Davies (adopted in 1845)
1842 Iefan William Davies
1843 Morgan Harrow Davies
1843 Sadie Hedley Davies (adopted in 1845)
1846 Bronwen Natasha Davies
1848 Alice Thomasina Davies (adopted at birth)
1849 Catrin Elise Davies

And their children:

Natasha and Raymond Devlin

Viscount Marblethorpe

1857 Vaughn Elis Devlin (Raymond's heir)
1861 Richard Seth Devlin

Lilly and Jasper Thomsett

1862 Seth Eckhard Thomsett (heir)
1863 Elise Marie & Anne Louise Thomsett
1864 George Jasper Thomsett (stillborn)

Chapter One

Princess Annalies Benedickta Davies of the royal Saxe-Coburg-Weiden dynasty rested the back of her trembling hand against her fine brow. "Perhaps it is impossible for a princess to raise children by herself. I don't know, anymore. The books lay it out perfectly and sensibly. I have both of you as inspiring examples of motherhood, yet I think…I suspect…I have failed as an ordinary mother."

Natasha rested on the ottoman in front of Annalies' chair, the twenty-five yards of tartan skirt of her dress spread around her like petals of a colorful flower. Annalies wondered if, hidden beneath the hoops, Natasha had her limbs arranged comfortably in an unladylike pose. From the waist up, she was a most elegant lady. A beautiful one, too. Natasha seemed to grow more lovely with each passing year.

"There is nothing ordinary about you, Anna," Natasha said, resting her hand on the Princess', where it lay limp on the arm of the wing chair.

"Exactly," Annalies replied, with not a trace of pride. "I cannot fulfill a simple biological function of womanhood. Bronwen is *completely* out of hand. Look at her."

Natasha studied Bronwen, the subject of their discussion. Anna's daughter sprawled on the big armchair on the other side of the big room. She sat with her legs draped *over* the arm of the chair. The arrangement was only possible because she wore no hoops and no corset. She *bent* in the middle.

Worse, the feet she swung, her heels kicking the side of the chair with every arc, were quite bare. Her pink toes peeped beneath the dirty hem of her petticoat.

Bronwen's hair, which was perhaps her best feature, if one did not first notice her clear gray eyes, was thick and long, ending well beneath her waist. Annalies knew the exact length because Bronwen had not bothered to pin it up. It hung free, only the side sections swept up to the back of her head. Bronwen would have arranged it that way for convenience's sake and no other reason.

There was not a single bow anywhere on Bronwen's ensemble. Not a scrap of lace, no embroidery, not a hint of embellishment. The buttons were plain bone things. Annalies suspected one or more of the buttons on her bodice might be missing. She was too afraid to look closely, for the confirmation would overwhelm her with despair.

"How could she let herself descend to such…such…" Annalies said, her throat tight.

"Freedom?" Natasha asked. "She's still young, Anna. Yes? Nineteen, I calculate?"

Anna pressed her lips together. "You were married at nineteen. Elisa was a mother at nineteen." She glanced at Elisa, who did not react. "Elisa, are you even listening?"

Elisa sat on the upright chair on Annalies' other side, her knees together and her skirt pooling around her boots, her hands together in her lap. She peered about the busy, crowded room.

Then she stirred. "Hmm?" She turned her head as if she was loath to look away. "Excuse me?" She frowned, her gaze turning inward for a heartbeat. "I was listening!" she protested, her frown clearing.

"Then it was not Bronwen you were studying so closely?" Natasha said.

Elisa smiled. It was a small expression, heated with emotion. "I am afraid you have both caught me indulging in motherly pride. I do apologize, Anna. It will seem as though I am trying to rub it in, only I cannot help watching the three of them and…oh, I am just so *pleased*!"

"The three of whom?" Anna asked. For the first time, she yanked her gaze away from her wayward daughter and cataloged the family members in the big room.

There was only one grouping of three among the couples and large circles of people laughing and talking and taking afternoon tea. Travers and his men were still to reach Anna's side of the room with their trays of tea, sugar and cream, and the plate of scones and pots of jam. They had not yet served the little group of three, either.

Ben kept company with Sharla and her husband, the Duke of Wakefield. All three stood together, intent on their conversation. Sharla watched Wakefield's face as he spoke, a small smile on her glowing face. Ben was also listening. His arm was about Sharla's waist.

As Wakefield finished speaking, the three of them laughed. Ben rested his other hand on Wakefield's shoulder, a comradely gesture. Wakefield tugged at the ribbon bow

Sharla wore at her neck, arranging it properly, before patting it into place. They were all intimate, familiar touches.

Anna's heart squeezed.

"All *three* of them?" she whispered, her throat clamping so she could barely breathe.

Natasha turned, peering.

Elisa shook her head. "No, no. Ben and Sharla are together. Wakefield is part of it, only…not." Her cheeks grew pink.

"Why not?" Anna demanded.

Elisa rolled her eyes.

Natasha laughed. "Because…well, think about it, Anna."

Anna felt the jolt down to her bones. "Oh…!" she breathed, studying Wakefield once more. "Who would ever have guessed?"

"I think that is the point," Natasha said. "No one is supposed to guess at all. At least, not outside the family, yes, Elisa?"

"Inside the family, we do as we please," Elisa finished. "And their arrangement pleases them very much. Just look at them. I've never seen any of them happier."

Anna took in Ben's relaxed pose. His arm about Sharla. The warmth and peace in his dark eyes. Yes, Elisa was right. "Ben asked to speak to me and Rhys after tea," Anna said. "Now I know why."

"You are pleased for him, aren't you?" Natasha asked, with an anxious note.

Anna considered it. "Yes," she said. "I believe I am. It isn't a conventional arrangement, although if they're happy…"

"Ben is his mother's son," Elisa said. "Convention has never been a strong suit of yours. Why should it be his?"

"Which brings me right back to the problem child of the day," Anna replied, glancing at Bronwen again. Bronwen was eating her cream-ladened scone, her head back as she lowered the entire scone down into her mouth with patent relish.

Anna sighed. "This is my fault. I failed them as a mother."

"Nonsense," Elisa said. "Ben is happy after years of moping and anger. Bronwen will find her way. You must give her more than the usual amount of time. Your children are all as headstrong as you, Anna. Even your adoptees acquired your stubborn streak."

"Thank you, I think," Anna said. "Although if Bronwen *must* have time to find her way, I do wish she wouldn't do it quite so…publicly. Our family has always kept our messes private. Bronwen seems to be determined to cavort where everyone can see her disgrace."

"She wants to be just like her big sister Sadie, that is all," Natasha replied.

"Sadie is at least experimenting with life in America where no one cares," Anna replied.

A hand rested on Anna's shoulder, drawing her attention to behind the chair. Jasper smiled at her and withdrew his hand. "I apologize for eavesdropping. It wasn't my intention. I was standing to one side, waiting for Lilly to arrive."

"Lilly is upstairs with the twins?" Elisa asked.

"She should be done by now," Jasper said. "I interrupted, because I believe I can offer a temporary solution regarding Bronwen, Princess."

"I'm listening," Anna said. "At this stage, I will listen to anyone," she added.

Jasper crouched down next to the chair so all three women could see him without straining their necks. "I will not interpret that as literally as you spoke it."

Anna put her hands to her cheeks. "Oh, Jasper, of course I didn't mean it that way! I do apologize—"

He held up a hand, his eyes dancing. "Natasha is correct. You must give Bronwen time. She has had a privileged upbringing, yet she is the daughter of a princess and a commoner. It can be confusing. I speak from experience."

Anna nodded. "Yes, your father, the Archeduke of Silkeborg. We are second cousins, Jasper. My grandmother married your father's great grandfather."

"Aren't *all* the Continental families threaded together, if you go back far enough?" Elisa asked.

"Most likely," Anna admitted. "Although, again I must apologize, Jasper. It isn't until this moment I even made the connection."

"I grew up not speaking about my father," Jasper told her. "I find the habit hard to dismiss. It is not entirely your fault."

"You said you had an idea about Bronwen, Jasper?" Natasha asked.

Jasper's smile grew wicked. "On how to give her time while minimizing her reputation's destruction among society? Yes. Let Bronwen come and live with me and Lilly for a while."

Anna drew in a breath, hope flaring. "At Northallerton?"

"The house is more than big enough," Jasper said. "Even with Lilly and me, little Seth and the twins, we still rattle about the place. Another adult would be welcome company for Lilly, too. I spend far too many of my days placating angry Yorkshiremen."

"Bronwen could run wild in the north, Anna," Elisa added. "No one would take the slightest interest in her, there."

Anna looked once more at her daughter. Bronwen was drinking her tea, now, holding the cup without the saucer and catching drips with her other hand. Anna winced. "I accept, Jasper," she told him. "With my desperate and humble thanks."

"We'll take care of your daughter, Princess," Jasper replied. "They say the air in the Vale is a cure for many ills."

"I most certainly hope so," Anna said and sighed.

Chapter Two

As they topped the last rise, the view opened across the valley, all the way to the great York road, on the far side. Running toward the road was Bullamoor Road, which Bronwen and Agatha had been following from a distance. On Bullamoor Road a carriage was heading west, toward Northallerton. Vehicles were unusual. The road was always empty.

Bronwen glanced at Agatha, to see she was not too breathless. These long walks were her precious joy, only her health was not what it used to be.

Agatha, though, was peering at the road and the carriage on it. Her eyes were too weak to read, yet her sight was keener than Bronwen's over great distances. The corners of her eyes wrinkled as she peered. "It isn't moving."

Bronwen looked again. After staring for long moments, she realized the carriage had made no progress along the road. It was still in the same location where she had first spotted it. "We can go farther south, instead," she told Agatha. They had been heading for the moors on the other side of the York road, where they hoped to find wild garlic and the last of the bog rosemary before the frosts.

"We should see if they need help."

Bronwen laughed. "Help from us? We're two women."

"No one stops on the road that way unless they're

forced to it."

Bronwen scowled at the motionless carriage. It looked small and far away. "Are you sure?" Agatha didn't like dealing with other people. Although, other people didn't like dealing with her. Bronwen wasn't sure which had come first.

"Help is help. It's always welcome." Agatha hitched the bag on her back into a more comfortable position.

"They could move on before we get there," Bronwen pointed out, as they walked down the gentle slope. The dale between them and road was a patchwork of emerald paddocks, darker hawthorn hedges and three white-washed cottages. Black-faced Yorkshire sheep cropped under the warm noonday sun, their dirty woolen backs white flecks scattered over the fields, creating a tweed effect.

The warmth and the cloudless sky had driven Agatha to insist upon her long walk today. There were few warm days like this left in the year. Bronwen had learned to trust Agatha's weather-sense and had capitulated when Agatha insisted on walking despite the stiffness of her joints and the ache in her back.

Agatha showed no sign of stiffness now as they negotiated the slope. "If they're gone when we get there, then our way won't be blocked anymore, will it?" she said in her wavering voice.

Bronwen couldn't argue with Agatha's reasoning. She saved her breath for the walk, for Agatha increased their pace until they were both striding across the shorn grass, scattering sheep as they went. Agatha sometimes surprised

Bronwen with displays of energy more suited to a far younger woman. Her mind was always young and modern.

The carriage remained where it was, even as they climbed the slope toward the rutted road. As they drew closer, Bronwen recognized the vehicle. It was one of the local hacks, who plied his trade between Northallerton town, where the train from York passed through, and locations in the valley. The carriage was listing to one side.

As most local passengers walked to Northallerton and saved their coins, it meant whoever had rented the hack was a stranger to the district.

Bronwen could see why the coach was motionless. The far side wheel lay on the ground and the driver was fussing with the axle. The horse stood with hips cocked, his nose to the ground, nipping at the tufts of grass between the tracks.

There were no passengers walking about. Had they insisted upon remaining inside the carriage, even on a day like this? How odd.

Agatha eased herself under the last hawthorn hedge. Bronwen wriggled through the thin opening, then tugged her skirt back into place. She tossed her hair back over her shoulder.

Agatha nodded toward the driver.

Bronwen moved over to where he was bent over the end of the axle. "Did you lose the pin?"

The driver straightened, startled. He swore, bringing his hand to his chest.

Bronwen kicked at the wheel. "It looks whole."

The man glared at her from under his thick, silver

brows. "Bloody pin sheered right off. If I can get the other end out, then I can put a temporary pin in place and be on my way." He glanced from Bronwen to Agatha, who was hovering near the rear corner of the carriage. "Or I might be if you two'd be men. How on earth I'm supposed to get the wheel back on…"

"One thing at a time," Bronwen told him. "Get the remains of the pin out first."

He glared at her. He looked as though he was building up to a pithy reply.

"Where are your passengers?" Bronwen asked, deflecting his ire. Through the leaning window, she could see the carriage was empty.

The driver scowled again and jerked his head toward the trees on the other side of the road. "He be inside, taking… well, a moment to himself, so to speak."

"Just the one, then. Well, let's look at the pin to start."

Agatha tugged on Bronwen's skirt. She turned her chin, toward the woods.

Bronwen heard the cracking and crunching of someone heavy moving through them. He was breathing hard. Harder than was justified for traversing a thin copse of ash trees that had lost most of their leaves.

Bronwen let her mouth curl down. He must be a London fop, unused to more exercise than lifting his brandy glass and knife and fork.

The man gasped. It was not a sound of exertion, but one of pain.

Bronwen started forward, toward the point where his

noisy progress told her he would emerge from the trees. As she got closer, he shouldered his way through the bare branches and fir trees, then staggered onto the verge at the side of the road.

He was a big man. That was the single impression Bronwen received before focusing upon his hand. He held the wrist tightly with the other hand, his fingers stretched taut.

Bronwen ran to him. "Let me see." She reached for his hand, intending to push the white, stiff cuff and thick worsted jacket sleeve out of the way.

"It *burns!*" he breathed and dug the fingers of his other hand into the skin over the back of the injured one.

Bronwen saw the telltale rash. Stinging nettle. Yes, he was in pain.

She looked through the trees, searching for the big, broad leaves of a dock plant and spotted one at the foot of an ash. "Agatha, the dock plant. Would you mind?"

Agatha nodded and stepped into the trees to harvest a leaf.

Bronwen returned her attention to the man's hand. He scratched with the other fingers. She slapped his hand away. "Don't do that."

His gaze met hers. Blue eyes, open wide in surprise. A blue that nature only provided not long before the sky turned to night black. "I beg your pardon?" he said, shocked.

"You'll just make it worse, if you scratch. Hold your breath for moment and leave it alone." She took his wrist and bent it, turning his hand over to see the palm and the underside of the fingers, looking for more burrs. "Did you brush your hand against the nettle when you were walking?"

"I must have. I don't remember. My hand suddenly burned. It is the most excruciating…what is that?" he finished sharply, looking at the moist, green leaf Agatha held out to Bronwen.

"Relief," Bronwen told him, taking the leaf.

"*Another* plant?"

She didn't answer. Instead, she turned his hand back over and wrapped the big leaf over the rash. There were no burrs left in his skin to remove. It must have been the lightest of contacts.

Bronwen held the leaf down with her fingers for a moment and watched him.

His expression was one of bewilderment and dismay. Then the dock leaf worked. She watched relief and growing awareness fill his face. His eyes met hers once more. "The pain is fading."

"Yes."

"That is extraordinary."

"Not really." She tapped the leaf. "Here, you can hold it in place. Leave it there for as long as you can." She let go of his wrist and braced herself for the usual suspicion and fear to settle into his eyes. *Witch* was the least of the epithets leveled at her in the past. People didn't trust what they didn't understand.

His gaze shifted from her to Agatha. For a heartbeat she saw Agatha as a stranger would: An old woman with long, stringy gray hair, a wrinkled face and few teeth. A back bent from carrying burdens far beyond what any woman should bear. And a patience and immoveable will rising from a long lifetime lived alone.

Bronwen squared her shoulders, ready to spring to Agatha's defense. It wouldn't be the first time.

The man looked at the dock leaf once more. "What is in the leaf?" he asked. "Something that counters the nettle sting, clearly, but what? What is the effective ingredient? Do you know?"

Bronwen's surprise left her speechless.

His interested faded. "Unless it is merely an old wives' tale you have remembered, that happens to work?"

The dismissive note whipped Bronwen into responding. "There is an acid compound in dock plants."

"Not a base?" he replied, his interest lifting once more. "I'd have thought that to counter such a sting, a base would be needed."

"It's not a sting. It's a burn. Mild acids alleviate that pain. If I'd had vinegar to hand, I could have used that, instead."

"Then you know your chemicals," he replied.

"As you do, apparently," she shot back.

For a moment, they looked at each other.

He had thick, golden blonde hair above the blue eyes and was clean-shaven. His clothes were fine gentlemen's garments, with a hint of European tailoring. His shoulders were wide, which matched his height and the size of his hand. The wrist she had glimpsed beneath the cuff was strong, too, which made him far more physical a man than the elegant suit and overcoat and bespoke tailoring suggested.

His square chin dipped. "I confess I am at the outer limits of my knowledge of chemicals. I suspect you know more than I. I would not have thought to find a complimentary plant to counter the first one."

"Well, using dock plants *is* an old wives' tale," Bronwen admitted. "I wanted to know *why* it worked, so I learned."

He nodded. It was a small movement. "Because knowledge is how the world becomes a better place."

"I suppose, yes. I haven't thought of it that way."

"I have." His gaze was steady.

"Ah! Got the bastard," the driver cried. A sharp ringing of metal punctuated his exclamation.

He bent and picked up the sheered pin from beneath the sagging axle and tossed it into the trees and rubbed his hands together, pleased. "I've got a couple of railway dog spikes in the box back here, that I picked up around the station. One of those will do nicely." He headed for the back of the carriage and Bronwen heard the box creak open and the driver rummage in the gear inside.

She bent and picked up the edge of the wheel and brought it up onto its edge, then rolled it closer to the carriage. "Agatha, you must thread it onto the axle. I'm stronger than you."

Agatha sidled past the man and put herself in front of the wheel and nodded.

Bronwen let it go and moved to the rear of the carriage. The driver straightened up, the thick metal spike in his hand. She nodded. "Is that why you kept them?"

"Never thought I'd have to use one," he admitted, shoving it in his pocket. He reached under the corner edge of the carriage and looked at her. "Let's see how strong you are, missy."

Bronwen got her fingers under the edge and nodded.

"One...two...*three*," the driver breathed.

Bronwen hauled, her neck and shoulders straining, as the edge of the carriage bit into her fingers. It was shockingly heavy. The two of them lifted it only a few inches.

"I need five more inches!" Agatha said, her voice wavering.

Bronwen let the carriage go and sucked at her fingers. The driver sighed. "It was a long shot, anyway," he said, his tone kindly.

"Let's try again," Bronwen told him. "This time, though..." She hauled her skirt up and bunched a fold of it over her hands and fitted them beneath the edge of the carriage.

The passenger was staring at her, his wounded hand held against his chest, the other hand cradling it so he could keep the dock leaf in place. He seemed both shocked and amused at the sight of her petticoat. Bronwen didn't care. She hadn't had to care about such things for a long while. Besides, the only way the carriage and the man would leave would be if she and the driver could lift the carriage high enough to let Agatha fit the wheel back on the axle. Practicality demanded the indecency.

She looked at the driver and nodded once more.

"One…two…three."

They lifted, blowing heavily. The carriage raised another three inches.

"More!" Agatha cried. "More!"

Abruptly, the carriage raised up the necessary four inches.

Bronwen gasped.

The passenger leaned his head to one side, from around the corner of the carriage. He was bent in such a way she could tell he had his hands beneath the side of the carriage there. "If you can do it, so can I." He straightened, moving out of sight. "Can you get the wheel on now?" Bronwen heard him ask Agatha. There was no strain in his voice.

The carriage remained raised and steady, while Bronwen listened to the wheel being fitted back on the axle. She could feel the vibrations through her grip on the bottom of the carriage.

"Let it down," the passenger told them.

Bronwen lowered the weight, rather than letting go. The driver copied her.

The carriage settled back an inch or two, then stayed there.

"Bugger me…" the driver murmured to himself, standing back and watching the conveyance as if it would give way and sink once more if he looked away. Then he moved around the corner to look at the wheel, pulling out the dog spike as he went. "Let me at it. Let's get it locked in tight before it spills once more."

Bronwen brushed her skirt back into place. There were

stains on the front of it from the grime beneath the carriage and tears from pushing through hedgerows. Few people would see her before she returned home and there was still rosemary to gather.

She moved around the carriage to check how Agatha fared.

The passenger bent and picked up the fallen dock leaf and placed it back over his hand.

Agatha shook her gray hair back over her face and hunched back into her customary posture and shrugged the bag back into position against her shoulders. "We should hurry, before the rain gets here." She looked at Bronwen.

Bronwen nodded.

"It will rain?" the man said. He looked up at the clear sky. "Impossible."

"Not so much," the driver told him, hammering his fist against the flat head of the dog spike, working it into the hole left by the missing pin to secure the wheel. "She be the witch woman. Most folks around here say she's got magic. I don't know about that. If she says it's going to rain then I, for one, would put the hay in the stable."

Agatha bent even more, turning her shoulder to hide her face. Bronwen rested her hand on Agatha's trembling shoulder. "Let's go," she whispered.

Agatha nodded.

They headed for the trees, hurrying.

"A moment!" the man called out.

Bronwen ignored him.

"How do I thank you? I don't know your name!"

"That suits me just fine!" Bronwen yelled back, just before they made their escape into the trees.

Chapter Three

After all Baumgärtner's talk about the richness and well-founded roots of Northallerton, when the house itself hove into view, Tor felt disappointed.

It was an ordinary, humble building, not at all like the grand estates Tor had spotted while enduring the interminable train journey from Edinburgh. He examined the many-angled establishment as the carriage eased around the long, sweeping curve leading up to the entrance. The wide curve gave him a view of two sides of the building.

The house was a jumble of rooflines, planes and chimneys, the brown slate roof melding into brown stone walls almost seamlessly. There were six dormer windows running along the side of the house, the glass shining in the afternoon sun. Two wide, tall façades of stone featured at the front, between the sloping roof. Three dormer windows ranged between the towers.

There was a pleasing symmetry to the arrangement, even if it wasn't grand marble. Vines grew up the sides of the house, reaching for the roof. Most of the leaves had dropped.

The glimpse of the side of the house proved it was as long as it was wide. A conservatory hugged the length of the flank. Beneath the glass and black iron, Tor could see green leaves and bright flowers. Summer still lingered inside. It was a pleasing note.

The outbuildings and staff quarters hid behind ancient oak trees. He could see them through the trunks and bare branches. The buildings matched the main house—brown stone, brown slate and a welcoming wisp of smoke rising from the chimneys, speaking of warmth and crackling flames inside.

There was a domestic, peaceful air about the establishment that was novel. Tor decided that he liked it. For now, anyway.

The carriage came to a gentle halt on the gravel in front of the house. The driver had been delicate in his handling of the vehicle—no heavy braking, no sharp turns, nothing that would stress the wheel and its temporary pin.

As the carriage came to a stop, the butler emerged, tugging his jacket sleeves into place.

When Tor had first walked into the bewildering and complex Waverley Train Station in Edinburgh without a companion or servant at his side, he had been reminded that he was expected to open his own doors. He'd adapted quickly. Now, he thrust open the carriage door and stepped onto the gravel. He folded the dock leaf and pushed it into his pocket. He may need it later. The medicinal benefits of the plant were undeniable.

"I would speak to your master," he told the butler.

The man nodded. "Might I have a name to announce you with, my lord?"

"No," Tor said.

The man blinked. "Ah…very well, then, my lord. If you will follow me?"

Tor nodded.

The butler turned and marched back into the house.

The front door, which had seemed humble, was deceptively large. Tor realized how wide and tall it was only when he passed through.

The space beyond the door was laid with more natural stone, worn to a smooth shine from generations of feet treading upon it. Massive oak beams crossed overhead. To the right, stairs ran up to the second floor, bending back on themselves in the middle. On the landing, wood paneling and plaster were below high windows. The mullioned windows let in the sun, that made the red in the patterned runner winding up the stairs blaze.

The air was warm and comfortable.

"This way, my lord," the butler murmured.

The room Tor was shown into was a drawing room. A large fireplace held a fire, burned down to white glowing coals. There were signs of occupation. An embroidery box with the lid still open and the lady's sewing hoop resting against the rim. A book left on a table beside the big chair by the fire. And a more intriguing note—a toy soldier beneath the sofa, with just the black legs with their bright red stripe peeping out.

Tor had never seen a child's toy in an adult room before.

The tension that had been sitting between his shoulders since leaving Edinburgh eased. He was in a far different world from his own, which was just what he sought.

He moved over to the fire. There were few flames to warm him, although the banked coals put out a ferocious heat. Not that he was cold. He had not been cold since arriving in Britain, although the damp had a way of oozing through to his bones and making them ache.

After a few long minutes, Tor heard the sound of footsteps on the stones in the hallway. Murmurs.

The door opened and the man that Tor had to presume was Jasper Thomsett stepped through and shut it once more.

Tor examined him. Thomsett was the same height as Tor, which few men were. That was where any similarity ended. Thomsett had black, curly hair and black eyes, which he must have got from his mother. He was not as broad across the shoulders.

His chin, though…

Tor stirred. "You have my father's mouth and jaw."

Thomsett's lips parted. His eyes widened. "You are Edvard?"

"I apologize for arriving unannounced in this way," Tor said. "The decision was sudden and impulsive. I hope you don't mind."

Thomsett gathered his wits. He straightened his shoulders and moved toward the fire. "Not at all, your Highness, although I confess this is so unexpected I am reeling with astonishment." He stopped on the other side of the mantel shelf and studied Tor. "You have your father's eyes and hair."

"So I'm told," Tor said. "I prefer to think of them as my own."

Thomsett considered him. "I did not think the two of us

would ever meet."

"In a properly-ordered world, perhaps not." Tor rested his hand on the high shelf and stared at the flames. "I'm not sure why I'm here, Thomsett. As you can tell from the lack of retinue about me, it is not an official visit." He laughed. "Not even the cabbie knew who I was."

He thought once more of the woman who had tended to the nettle sting. Her direct look and commanding way. That had been as much of a shock to him as the expectation that he open his own doors. He could still feel the tingle on his hands and wrists from her touch and manipulations.

Such ability in a woman so young and so common needed further consideration.

Tor shook himself. Well, he had wished to escape his own world. Clearly, he had succeeded.

"Have you run away, then?" Thomsett said, his tone light.

"In a way."

Silence.

Tor glanced at him. "I was touring Scotland. We've been gone almost a year from Silkeborg, visiting Europe and beyond."

"I heard." Thomsett's smile was a ghostly thing. "Your life is reported in English papers, too."

"That must gall you," Tor said.

Thomsett's smile was complete this time and just as truthful. "I don't envy you your life for a moment, your Highness. Not one whit."

Tor nodded. "If you feel that way, then perhaps you understand why I am here. There has been a cholera outbreak in Scotland."

"That, I had not heard," Thomsett admitted. "It is bad?"

"Bad enough that Baumgärtner insisted we abandon the good will tour and move onto France. I agreed we must leave Scotland, only when it came to it, I couldn't abide another official visit." He glanced at Thomsett and away, stirring uncomfortably. "Baumgärtner calls it a good will tour. In reality, it is a wife hunt. At every turn, marriageable maidens are trotted out for me to inspect."

"Ah...." Thomsett's voice was full of sudden understanding. "Then Baumgärtner has not yet retired? I thought he might. He spoke of it when I was in Silkeborg, five years ago."

"He would see me married and an heir to secure the title, before considering it. Only, I suspect Baumgärtner thought it would be a matter of months, not years. I have been trying his patience. This tour has been an abrasive reminder of my failure. I could stomach no more of the parade."

Thomsett did not respond at once. He turned and looked into the glowing coals. "You may not enjoy being reminded of how similar you are to your father, your Highness, but your impatience is very much like him. My mother told me many times how the yoke of responsibilities and duties chafed him."

"While *my* mother told me how well his army uniform fit him, the day they met."

"Was that not the day they wed?" Thomsett asked, his

tone gentle.

"Precisely. She could not look at his face the entire day." Tor sighed. "I will not say I envy you your childhood because, frankly, I do not. You were raised a bastard in a country that does not treat bastards kindly. Yet you got the better half of my father—his goodwill and his…love."

"You had him in your life." Thomsett gave an impatient wave of his hand. "We could stand here arguing losses on both sides all day. There is no point. It is what it is. If you are running away, your Highness, then you have come here to hide?"

"Frank words." Tor hesitated. "Do you mind my landing upon you and yours in this way? I cannot bring myself to think of it as hiding, even in my mind. I would appreciate a moment to…draw breath. I am not sure how long that moment may last. Baumgärtner will find me soon enough."

"Sooner than that," Thomsett replied. "He's a wily Swiss. Will he not raise an alarm? He could turn the country inside out, looking for you."

"I left a note that will delay that reaction," Tor told him. "He knows I've left of my own free will. He just doesn't know where I've gone. With the Scotland leg of the tour canceled because of the cholera outbreak, my next formal engagement is a month away. He won't panic until closer to that date."

Thomsett bent and picked up the poker and stirred the fire to life. Then he laid a log from the copper basket sitting upon the corner of the hearth onto the coals and watched it catch fire. "You are welcome to the hospitality of my home, your Highness, although you may find my company more uncomfortable than the maidens you avoid. We do not know each other at all, despite being united by a single father."

"That is a risk I must take, although if I can withstand the company of Silkeborg's mayor and his councilors, I can surely suffer through yours."

Thomsett smiled. "Then I must put you in the room with my tenant farmers and see how long you last with them."

"Ah, yes. Baumgärtner told me about the qualifying clause in my father's will. He was impressed by your handling of the matter."

Thomsett pushed his hands into his pockets. "If it is your intention to breathe, as you say, then you cannot be a guest here as yourself." Thomsett waved toward the window. "It only looks as though there are miles of fields and sheep out there. In fact, this district is a writhing mass of gossips. If word escapes that an Archeduke is staying at Northallerton, it will spread at a speed greater than the London Express. You will have Baumgärtner here on the doorstep inside two days."

"I see…" Tor *did* understand. This was the first time in his life he had been completely alone. It was a heady sensation to walk by himself, unremarked and almost invisible. He'd strolled among trees and heard only his own footsteps. He had stood by the side of a country road and witnessed a silence so complete that the movement of a bird far inside the trees was loud in comparison. He had experienced all of it only by hiding his real identity. That shield must remain in place for such moments to continue. "I could not claim you as my brother, if I am to lie about who I am. You have ensured the world knows who your father is."

"You can claim to be a distant cousin." Thomsett said. "The Princess Annalies, who is my honorary aunt, actually *is* a cousin to both of us. You would not be lying, your Highness."

"If I am to be a distant cousin, then you must stop using my title."

"What should I call you then?" Thomsett asked. "'Lorensburg' would be just as revealing as 'your Highness'."

"Your family—the extended family, I mean—Baumgärtner explained to me the practice you have of using each other's first names, within the family."

"I should call you Edvard?"

Tor winced. "That is what my mother called me."

"What do your closest friends call you, then?" Thomsett hesitated. "You don't have close friends," he finished.

"None with the degree of intimacy that allows the use of personal names," Tor admitted. "My father…" It was his turn to hesitate. His father was Thomsett's father and Thomsett already resented that the man had been absent in his life.

Thomsett's eyes narrowed. "He used a different name?"

"The one name he was permitted to choose for me, after the committee had finished their selections. Tor."

"Tor." Thomsett tried it softly. "Edvard Christoffer…

are there any more in there?"

"Adam for my grandfather. Bernhardt for my mother's father."

"Edvard Christoffer Adam Bernhardt Tor Lorensburg."

Tor shook his head. "No one has ever strung them together in that way before."

"It is the common man's practice," Thomsett replied. "I have the right to call myself Jasper Anson Dominik of Northallerton, or even just Northallerton, although people in these parts would look at me oddly if I did."

"Dominik," Tor repeated, startled. "He gave you his own name?"

Thomsett's gaze met his. "That was all I was given."

Tor made himself breathe away the tiny note of resentment chiming in his chest. "You spoke truly, a moment ago. We could challenge each other for a month on our respective losses and wounds, if we wanted to."

Thomsett stirred and stepped away from the fire. "I and my family will call you Tor. The rest of the world can call you…Besogende."

Tor smiled. Thomsett's accent was not quite right, yet clear enough to recognize the Danish. "I *am* a visitor, after all." He could feel the fluttering of warmth in his chest and middle. It was not from the fire, but from the idea that a tiny group of people—Thomsett's family alone—would use his father's name for him.

It pleased him.

Thomsett glanced at the carriage clock on the mantel shelf. "Your trunks are outside?"

"I packed a valise. The driver would have given it to your butler, I suppose." He frowned. "Should I have carried it myself?"

"Warrick would have seen to it." Thomsett tugged on the bell pull next to the fire. "Afternoon tea approaches. I will introduce you to Lilly. Afterward, you must meet Seth and the twins." Thomsett cocked his head. "Do children bother you?"

"I wouldn't know," Tor said. "I don't think I've ever spoken to one directly."

Thomsett shrugged. "We don't keep our children in the nursery all day. You'll learn quickly enough how to deal with them."

Tor glanced at the toy soldier on the floor beneath the sofa once more. "It is all very new to me," he admitted. He met Thomsett's gaze. "Newness pleases me."

Thomsett put his hand to his temple, as if he had just remembered something. "Oh lord, Bronwen…" He dropped his hand and straightened. "You most likely won't meet Bronwen until supper tonight. If then." He gave a self-conscious laugh. "You say newness pleases you, only Bronwen will test your resolve, your…Tor."

Tor shook his head. "The newer, the better," he said firmly.

"You say that now," Thomsett replied as the butler, Warrick, stepped into the room. "Wait until supper," he added, his tone one of warning.

Chapter Four

Jasper arrived not long after Fisher had brought Lilly the extra blanket from the linen press and tucked it around her legs.

Jasper dropped to his knee next to the *chaise longe* Lilly lay upon and kissed her. It was a warm, slow kiss, that made her heart stir and her body to tighten.

Then, with a regretful expression, he settled back and brushed a stray hair from her cheek. His gaze moved over her face.

"I am well," she assured him, answering his unspoken question. "I am tired, though. We've been back from Cornwall for a week and I cannot sleep enough. I don't know why. This year's Gathering was placid compared to some years."

Jasper smiled, only it didn't reach his eyes. "The usual hell-raisers were not on hand this year. They've scattered about the world on their adventures." He picked up her hand, his fingers warm and strong. "You've been through a physical ordeal that would tax even strong men, Lilly. Give yourself time."

Lilly thought of the tiny new grave in the family plot, at the top of the dale. Her throat tightened and her eyes stung. She wiped them with her free hand. "I'm sorry. I do this even with the most lateral of references…"

Jasper cupped her cheek. Pain showed in his eyes. "Me,

too," he admitted. "I know a man should not admit to that, but I do. No one has caught me at it, yet, although there have been close calls. I miss George, too."

"He wasn't with us for more than a day, yet there is a hole here." She touched her chest.

Jasper's hand squeezed hers. "I may have found a distraction for you."

"Beyond Bronwen's escapades?" Lilly asked.

"Where *is* Bronwen, anyway?" Jasper asked. "I checked in the library on the way upstairs. She isn't at her usual spot."

"On the ladder?" Lilly smiled, despite the aching in her chest. "How on earth she finds perching upon a hard ladder comfortable when there are perfectly good armchairs within reach is beyond me. If she is not in the library, then she is most certainly out walking. Possibly with Agatha, if the poor woman is up to it. I hope they don't get wet."

Jasper glanced through the window. "It is cloudless out there."

"Look at the horizon. There's rain coming," Lilly assured him.

"I will take your word for it," Jasper replied, glancing through the window once more and frowning.

"And the distraction?"

Jasper hesitated. She felt small tension build in him.

"What is it?" she asked.

"My brother is here."

Lilly stared at him. For a moment, she could not think of who Jasper's brother might be. Jasper was a bastard and alone in the world.

Then the necessary facts came to her.

Lilly tried to sit up. "The Archeduke of Silkeborg is in the drawing room? You *left* him there?" Horror spilled through her. "Jasper, my God! You can't leave the room without a royal's permission! You must go back. Now."

"I know the protocol," Jasper told her. Warmth and humor were building in his eyes. "Actually, he's no longer in the drawing room. He's in the second-best guest room, where Warrick put him."

"The *second* best?" Lilly cried, alarm forcing her up and bringing her feet to the floor, in a tangle of mohair and tartan.

Jasper laughed. "Bronwen has the best room. I suppose Warrick didn't want to turn her out."

"What is he thinking?" Lilly said, trying to untangle the blanket from the flounces on her dress and her heels. "Of *course* Bronwen must vacate the room. One doesn't offer royalty anything but the best one has."

Jasper unwound the blanket and dropped it on the green velvet next to her. "While Tor is here, he does not want to be royal at all. Warrick thinks he is a distant cousin, visiting from Denmark. Tor Besogende."

Lilly grew still, absorbing Jasper's extraordinary statement. She could feel her eyes widen.

Jasper picked up her hand again and held it between his two warm ones. "I don't know how to explain it. I don't have the full details. I don't know the man, yet the sensation I got from talking to him for just a few minutes...it was odd, Lilly. I kept thinking he's just like us. He's reeling, looking for something to hold on to while he finds his way forward."

Lilly's chest ached. "The poor man," she breathed. "We must surely be able to help him while he is here, Jasper."

"I would not put it so boldly to Tor," Jasper advised her. "He has the same prickly pride Annalies sometimes displays."

"The haughty look she gives, when the strangest things offend her?" Lilly asked.

"Exactly."

Lilly squeezed his hand. "My God, Jasper…Bronwen!"

Jasper shook his head. "I've been worrying how he might react to Bronwen. Only, I think—I suspect—Bronwen's ways might be just the cure he's looking for."

"We're used to her, Jasper. Tor—is that what we're to call him? Tor is not used to anything but the most genteel and mannered people. He'll be shocked by her. Maybe even disgusted."

"Shocked, perhaps. A man who manages to pack his own valise and travel through a strange country by himself when he's never done either…that sort of man has a resilience that will not let him descend to disgust."

Lilly considered it. "As distractions are measured, Jasper, I think you may have outdone yourself with this one. The next little while will be very interesting."

* * * * *

It had taken days of shouting before Bronwen had conceded and promised that, no matter what she might get up to during the day, she would present herself at dinner and attempt to be civilized for the duration of the meal.

Lilly's pale face, the first time Bronwen had stayed out in the woods for the night, had been a shock to Bronwen, as had Jasper's ringing, scathing tirade about responsibility, respect and empathy. He had been as worried as Lilly, a fact that had only made itself known to Bronwen *after* she had scared them silly.

Bronwen always made her way back to Northallerton if she was out, now. She would arrange to arrive before the dinner hour so she could wash and dress in her one presentable gown. Sometimes, she even tried to pin her hair up, although most of the time, she did not bother.

Nor did she bother this evening. The rain had caught her as she had been walking home after seeing Agatha was warm and comfortable in front of the fire pit in her little one-room cott, next to the Willow Beck. Bronwen had left the rosemary with Agatha to prepare for drying, up in the roof of the cottage.

Because her hair was damp, Bronwen left it loose rather than fight to pin it in a simple coil, the most she ever bothered with. She glanced at her muddy boots and left them off, too. The floor in the house was always warm underfoot, except for the slate in the front hall.

Lilly had hemmed Bronwen's calico gown and her petticoats so she could wear them without hoops and not trail the hems along the ground. That made the wearing of them considerably more comfortable.

She didn't bother looking in the mirror. The same plain, unremarkable face would stare back at her as usual. Instead, she went downstairs to the drawing room. Even though this was backwater Northallerton, Jasper and Lilly still insisted upon a civilized *apéritif* and conversation before dinner was announced.

It had taken more weeks for Bronwen to understand that they insisted upon the formality because they liked to hear about her days and how she filled them. Nothing shocked either of them and Bronwen had stopped trying. That was when she learned the one thing that terrified them was unnecessary risks that threatened her well-being. Outside that single limit, Bronwen was free to do as she pleased.

As Bronwen was not interested in risking body and soul, either, it was an arrangement everyone had grown used to.

When she reached the drawing room, Bronwen saw Lilly was sitting on the end of the sofa, as usual. Jasper was beside her. He had hovered close to her since the loss of George.

Bronwen let out a soft sigh at the reminder.

There was a third person in the drawing room. The man remained seated in the wing chair by the fire, holding a sherry glass in his big hand and staring at the flames. He turned his head as she entered and Bronwen came to a confused halt by the pianoforte.

It was the passenger she had tended on Bullamoor Road that morning. His eyes widened just as Bronwen could feel her own eyes doing.

Jasper got to his feet, as polite and formal as always, even though Bronwen didn't care about such matters. He glanced at the man in the wing chair and gave a tiny gesture with his hand.

The man rose to his feet and cleared his throat. He looked at Jasper expectantly.

Bronwen did, too.

"Bronwen, may I present to you Master Tor Besogende, from Denmark. He is a distant cousin of mine. Tor, this is Miss Bronwen Natasha Davies, daughter of Princess Annalies of the royal house Saxe-Coburg-Weiden and the Honorable Rhys Davies, of London."

Tor Besogende hesitated, then bent in a bow. "Miss Davies."

Startled, she nearly curtsied back. His bow was stiff and regal and unexpected in a commoner. "Mr. Besogende," she acknowledged, struggling to pronounce his name correctly. "Are you staying at Northallerton?"

"I am," Besogende confirmed. "I hope that does not inconvenience you…or anyone here."

"Jasper and Lilly cope with my comings and goings. I'm sure you'll be a simple guest in comparison," Bronwen told him.

His brow lifted. "No one ever finds my company simple."

Bronwen almost laughed. The arrogance of the man!

Lilly got to her feet. "Perhaps you should introduce Tor properly," she told Jasper. "It would allow Tor to relax, if he doesn't have to remember who knows what."

"Tor?" Jasper said.

Bronwen looked from one man to the other. There was a resemblance there, about the mouth and chin, enough to tell her they were related in some fashion.

Why was Jasper deferring to his cousin, though? He was the head of the family.

Tor sighed and nodded. "Your lady-wife is correct. It would be easier to not have to guard my every word."

Bronwen frowned. "Guard against what, precisely?"

Lilly's smile had a measure of wickedness in it.

Bronwen looked at Jasper once more.

Jasper held out his hand toward Besogende, frowning. "I can't introduce you formally."

Lilly sighed and stepped forward. "Let me do it. Then there is no formal recognition. Bronwen, Tor is Jasper's brother. His *half* brother, to be precise."

Bronwen frowned. "Only, your brother is…the Archeduke Edvard Christoffer…"

Besogende's brow lifted. "At your service," he murmured and bent in another low bow.

"Oh…" Bronwen breathed, stunned.

"While he is staying here, Bronwen, Tor will be just Tor Besogende to everyone."

"Why on earth would you want to do that?" Bronwen asked him.

Tor looked startled. He glanced at Jasper. For help or guidance, or perhaps both.

Jasper just smiled.

Tor cleared his throat. "I…suppose…because I grew

weary of the unceasing predictability of my life."

"You're an Archeduke. Can't you just wave your hand and demand it change and it is done?"

Jasper's smile grew. Even Lilly was amused.

Bronwen realized she was yet again too forward, her speech too blunt. Only, it was too late. She had spoken. So she lifted her chin and waited for Tor to answer.

He rubbed the back of his neck. "I think you misunderstand the intricacies of royal life."

"I'm half royal," Bronwen shot back. "I have arranged my life to suit me. Why can you not?"

"It isn't that simple…"

"Why not?"

"I cannot just abandon my responsibilities and duties. A whole country of people would come to grief."

"You're in Northallerton, hiding behind a commoner's name. Does that not define abandoning your people?"

Tor's eyes narrowed. "You are direct, aren't you?"

"And you are avoiding answering my question."

"Bronwen…" Lilly breathed.

"No, Lilly," Jasper said. "If Tor wishes to be just Tor Besogende while he is here, he must get used to questions both blunt and direct and deal with everyone equally."

Tor held up his hand. "I will answer, although I suspect Miss Bronwen is far more blunt than the average Yorkshireman." He looked at her. "As I have no need to cling to royal graciousness, I will ask you a rude question of my own. You are the daughter of Princess Annalies. That station in life comes with expectations of its own. By your appearance and from your actions this morning, I can attest you are failing to meet those expectations at every turn. In fact, you appear to delight in *not* meeting them. Tell me why you shirk your duties, Miss Bronwen and I will tell you why I have put mine aside."

Bronwen's heart thudded. She stared at him, unable to pull together a reasonable answer. His attack had been swift and stunning.

His gaze was as steady as it had been that morning.

Bronwen licked her lips. "I find myself without appetite. Jasper, please excuse me from dinner."

She turned and left, moving as fast as her uncooperative limbs would allow.

"What happened this morning?" Lilly asked, behind her. She was not talking to Bronwen.

"You've met Bronwen before just now, Tor?" Jasper added.

"Briefly, on my way here…" Tor began.

Flouncing from the room had not stirred a single one of them, not even *him*.

Their indifference inflamed her. Bronwen stomped across the hall, until her bare foot came down upon a sharp pebble that had not yet been swept up. The sting was minor, yet her eyes filled with tears.

She hated crying. It was such a weak, womanly thing to do. That made her even angrier. With a soft cry of rage, she pulled up her skirt and petticoat and looped them over her arm, then ran up the steps two at a time and locked herself in her room.

Damn him.

Who did he think he was?

The Archeduke Edvard Christoffer of Silkeborg, her treacherous memory reminded her. Answerable to no one but himself.

"Not while he's here, he's not," she whispered to herself, rubbing her foot where the pebble had bit.

She would make him rue his masquerade. Oh, yes and she would *like* doing it.

Chapter Five

"Why on earth they must start these things in the middle of the night is beyond me," Jack muttered, fussing with his cloak. His hood fell back again.

Cian yanked the fronts of the cloak back into place for him. "They've been doing it this way time out of mind. No one will change it now. Anyway, it's only nine in the evening. You make it sound as though midnight has come and gone."

"Palmerston isn't a royal. It's the Queen who decided he should get a state funeral. While she was deciding that, you'd think she'd decide to hold it at a convenient time."

Cian might have made a jest about Jack's sour mood, except that Jack had been in a sour mood for well over a year. Everyone in the family knew why, so no one teased him about it.

"We're so far back in the line," Jack added, glancing across the length of the Horse Guards Parade. "You're an earl for heaven's sake." He pulled his hood back up over his face. "We're in an alley at the back end of the procession. It's dark as pitch here. I can't see what I'm doing."

It was true they were at the tail end of the funeral procession, which was ready to move forward. The casket would emerge through the tunnel at any moment, although they were so far away from the head of the procession they would not see it. However, they were not the only ranking peers standing about the alley in their cloaks and hoods, waiting to begin. There were dukes and petty princes among them, too.

When royalty from across Europe, heads of state and peers had come to pay their last respects to England's Prime Minister, mere earls of the realm must come last.

The light was a different matter. Cian glanced at the flickering gas lamps that lined the narrow alley. They were flaring and dimming with irritating irregularity, sending shadows leaping and making the horses skittish. A line of private family carriages waited along the alley, for no one could leave their conveyances directly in front of the Parade. There simply wasn't room.

"There must be something in the gas, making them jump in that way," Jack said.

"An impurity. It happens," Cian said.

The line of the carriage closest to the nearest lamp was familiar to him. Cian's heart squeezed as he studied the shield on the door. Gainford's coach.

Once before he'd examined the coach and raised his gaze to find Eleanore looking at him. She would not be in the empty, darkened coach tonight, yet he still lifted his gaze to the glass in the door.

Eleanore was there, watching him.

Cian's breath evaporated. His heart rocked.

She was here, the last place he would expect her to be. She had not said she would be, in her last letters, although the funeral had been arranged quickly.

As his gaze met hers, Eleanore pressed her fingers to the

glass.

Cian knew she had come out tonight not to keep her father company, but on the chance she might see Cian. That daring was in her blood, a part of her.

There were too many people around them who knew both Cian and her for him to risk approaching the carriage openly. She would know that, too.

Eleanore gave him one of her heated smiles, the one that made his belly crimp and his innards to tangle. His pulse, already unsteady, spiraled upward.

Jack said something.

Cian fought to calm his breath, to reveal nothing.

"I said, it's started," Jack growled. He tugged on Cian's cloak, coaxing him to turn away, to face in the direction the procession was moving.

The line of gas lamps along the alley flared once more, the brightness chasing away the shadows. Farther down the alley, a lamp exploded with a bang and a woofing sound as the gas escaped into the night air and ignited. Glass tinkled on the cobbles below, as people gasped and reared backward.

Horses whinnied and shuffled. Coach wheels squealed as the horses' movements twisted and scraped them over the cobbles.

Then the lamp closest to the Gainford coach exploded.

Jack winced and ducked, as did most of the cloaked figures around them.

The gray mare reared, her eyes rolling. Her hooves pawed the air, then landed, sending up sparks. That further alarmed the creature and she bolted.

Cian glimpsed Eleanor's wide eyes, her hand clutching at the grab rail, as she tumbled backward in the carriage.

There was no thought in it. No decision. Cian ran after the carriage as it rattled down the alley, causing the cloaked men to scatter in alarm. Their cries and shouts added to the horse's terror. The coach picked up speed.

Cian had been rather good at track and field at college. He had the long legs that gave him a competitive edge and he was fast. He gave it his all, now. It was still early enough in the evening that the night mist had not set in. The cobbles were not slippery yet, which gave him the extra power he needed for a burst of speed that put him within reaching distance of the rocking carriage. He leapt and caught at the top of the luggage shelf railing and hung on.

The carriage picked up speed as the horse took the sharp corner at the end of Horse Guards Road, careening down Great George street. There were no other carriages, no cloaked figures here. The echo of the rattling carriage bounced off the buildings, which would not reassure the mare or give it reason to slow.

Cian tugged at the ties at his throat and let the wind of their passage tear the cloak from his shoulders. Then he climbed up onto the rack. The Gainsford coach was a hard-topped model, which allowed him to climb over it and onto the driver's bench. It was difficult, for the carriage was rocking and swaying wildly. He stayed down low, easing his way forward until he could drop onto the cushion on the driver's bench with a gusty sigh of relief. His lungs were bellowing and his heart slamming in his chest.

He untied the reins and hauled on them. "Whoa!" he cried, as the horse bucked the command. He stamped on the brake lever and heard the brake scrape against the wheels. The wheels were the new and expensive iron-rimmed type. The grinding of metal against metal didn't reassure the horse.

As they clattered over Westminster Bridge, the fog sitting on the river swirled over them. The horse fought Cian's commands, too unnerved to obey.

It took a long ninety seconds for the horse to calm and the carriage to slow to a stop. Cian threw himself to the ground and hurried around to the mare's nose and patted and crooned until its eyes stopped rolling.

By then, Eleanore had the carriage door open and eased herself to the ground.

Cian gave the horse a last pat and hurried to where she clung to the door. "Are you hurt?"

She brushed her satin evening gown back into place with trembling hands. "I am shaking, that is all. Oh, Cian!"

He couldn't help it. He had to hold her. He pulled her against him and kissed her.

It was only the second kiss he'd dare to take, yet her lips felt like the touch of a familiar lover. She *was* familiar to him, as dear as a longtime companion and friend. They had never lingered in the same room together, even at the innumerable public functions they both attended, although they were the closest of friends.

For two years they had been writing to each other at

least twice a day. Via paper and ink, Cian had learned more about Eleanore's thoughts and feelings, her hopes and her fears about the future, than he could have ever hoped to have learned through formal conversations.

Her lips tasted just as he remembered, just as he thought they should. Eleanore flowed against him, pliant and willing, heated and eager.

His body tightened, leaping to the ready with an eagerness he'd never experienced before.

Cian groaned and tore his lips from hers. "Enough. Enough, for now."

Eleanore rested her hand on his chest. Through the fabric of his shirt and waistcoat and jacket, he could feel the heat of that light touch. It was a brand, leaving a permanent mark upon his soul. She looked up at him with her warm, brown eyes. There was knowledge there. Understanding.

"Can we go somewhere? There's no one here to see us. Oh, Cian, even just a few minutes alone…how wonderful that would be!"

He swallowed and glanced around. They were on the other side of the Thames, close to Waterloo Station. There were numerous hotels and inns about the station, catering to travelers.

It was a risk, but then, they had known all along that their association was dangerous. They had discussed it in their letters. Because neither of them could bear to give up even that small contact, they had ignored it.

"Get back in the carriage," he told her, reaching behind her to hold open the door. "There's an inn, just up the road."

Her smile was a simmering reward.

* * * * *

Tor sat upon the tufted coverlet on the bed. He would not sleep beneath a silk quilt tonight. It was not even a quilt that lay over the sheets. It was a blanket made of wool yarn that had been knitted or worked in some English way so the patterns twisted about each other, forming braids and leaves and flowers.

There was no light in the room, except for the flood of moonlight coming in the window. If he wanted light, he must light the lantern on the table beside the bed himself. If he wanted the window open, he must open it himself, despite not being sure *how* to open it.

What was he doing here? The hellion tonight had been right to challenge him. He'd been selfish, escaping here. He had forgotten that decisions he made affected more people than himself.

Only he *had* thought it through. He had spent a sleepless night beneath a silk quilt, debating the consequences of stealing this brief, unanticipated pocket of time for himself.

Silkeborg was in good hands. Baumgärtner, with his assistants in Denmark, managed affairs via the efficient postage system available in Europe now, along with the marvelous wire telegraph for lightning fast communications.

The hellion had not asked him that, nor clarified the details of his departure from Scotland. She had simply accused him of recklessness.

In all his life, Tor had never struck back the way he had done with her. It had taken Jasper's reminder that he *could* disregard the restrictions of his station for him to shrug aside the habitual repression of his impulses and fire a personal challenge at her.

It had felt *good* to indulge himself in that petty freedom. At least, it had for perhaps three heart beats.

He'd seen hurt in her eyes. Surprise. He'd struck deep, exactly as he had hoped. Only, it no longer felt like a victory.

Tor sighed and looked at the ghostly shine of light pouring through the window once more.

He had made a mistake.

Was the mistake striking out at a defenseless woman? Or was it greater than that? Was the mistake coming here in the first place?

* * * * *

The Hog & Bramble had been built in the last century and had never modernized. Stepping into the main tavern was to step into the time of tri-corners and muskets, wenches and highwaymen. Given the inn's location by the river, on the other side from the heart of London, it catered to a rough clientele who valued their privacy. Many of the tables were tucked away in alcoves that could be made completely private by drawing curtains across.

Cian made sure the curtain was drawn so that anyone passing would not glimpse the occupant. Not that he wanted to have his way with a wanton lass, which was why the curtains had been placed there originally. Eleanore, however, was a woman who glowed with elegance and refinement. In this place, she drew the eye. She would be remembered.

Anyone who came after the runaway carriage would find it soon enough. Cian would have only moments after that. For now, though, they could steal a few precious moments together, uninterrupted.

Cian ordered a brandy for each of them. It would help Eleanore settle her nerves.

Cian's nerves needed soothing, too. It didn't help that Eleanore did not sit decorously on the other side of the table. Instead, she slid around the u-shaped bench, careless of the blue satin of her evening dress and settled herself close to his side. Cian could feel the heat of her against him.

He shivered and drank.

Eleanore put her hand on his wrist as he went to lift the glass a third time. It was a light touch, yet halted him as surely as an anchor.

He looked at her.

She touched his face. Her fingers curled over his jaw. "Kiss me," she pleaded. "We have little time. We can talk all we want later, as we have all this last year. Please kiss me."

He shuddered. "We shouldn't."

"We should not be corresponding as we have, either," she reminded him. "Shall we stop? Should I burn your letters when they come, from now on?" Her jaw was fine and as steady as her gaze. Her slender throat was straight, her shoulders square. There was no pleading in her. She was too proud for that.

Burn his letters? *No!* The silent cry was abject. Cian kissed her, instead.

The fire leapt between them. Instant heat, vaporizing all thought, all good sense, all the building despair about the future.

He had kissed many women in the past. Eleanore was different. Always, he expected to feel the iron core of her mind and the firmness of her soul that he had come to know through her letters. She was a rare woman, who knew her own mind and unbelievably, she wanted him, Cian Williams.

He thought that when he touched her, he would sense that strength in her. Instead, he tasted warm softness. She was pliable silk against his hands and body, driving him onward.

He lets his lips trail to her throat, down to her bare shoulders, where he lingered, stoking her flesh with his mouth, as she moaned against him and arched her back, inviting more exploration. Her hands moved in his hair, then dropped to his chest and slid beneath his jacket. The light touch scorched him wherever it roved and made the coil of tension in his belly tighten and harden.

When his hand cupped the mound of her breast, she merely gasped and pressed herself into him.

Cian closed his eyes and grew still, listening to the throb of his body and the rapid beat of his heart. Her ragged breath. Her soft sigh.

He lifted his head and looked at her. "It would be too

easy to let this progress to where we both know it is going."

She swallowed and nodded. "I want you. I know a lady isn't supposed to want that, only I do. I *ache* with it, Cian. Only, I know I would hate myself and even you, a little, if we did."

He tightened his hands about her waist. "Marry me," he said. "We can elope. Ireland—I have an estate there. Once we are married, no one can gainsay the binding, not even your father."

Her eyes glistened with tears she would not let fall. "I would dishonor the family. I would insult the prince. My father is a powerful man, Cian. He would make your life unbearable. You would be shunned by society."

"I don't care about any of that," Cian said roughly. "Nor do you."

"Only, it would put a stain on our marriage. No, Cian, don't look at me in that way. Tell me you could...could take me, with a clear conscience, knowing what it cost you and your family?"

Cian remained silent, seething.

She put her hand on his arm. Heat. Softness. His heart thudded harder.

"It isn't just you my father will ruin," Eleanore continued. "It is everyone dear to you. Even your Great Family is not beyond his reach. My father knows too many influential people. I've seen him do it, Cian. He is ruthless when he does not get his way."

"There must be a way we can be together," Cian growled.

"There is not. You have known that from when this began, or you would have confronted my father long ago."

He hung his head, breathing hard. She spoke nothing but the truth. They had been over and over this in their letters. Only, hearing her say it aloud in her beautiful, musical voice, made it hurt as if the wound was fresh.

This time, Eleanore kissed him, pressing herself up against him with a soft moan. Her sound of need inflamed his already aching body. He was burning with wanting. They twined together, as close as two people could become in such a place, their bodies meshed, flesh stroking flesh.

When Cian heard his name being called from the public room of the inn, he let her go and closed his eyes, trying to school his heart and contain himself. Anyone seeing him now would see the desperation surging through him.

"Cian! Where are you?" A male voice, one he recognized.

Cian opened his eyes. "Jack," he told Eleanore. "At least it is my cousin and not your father who came after us." He lifted his hand to the edge of the curtain.

Eleanore slipped her fingers over his wrist and pulled his hand away. She looked at him. A simple look, yet the emotion in her eyes as she studied his face, her gaze moving over it, told him everything she would not say.

"Cian…" she breathed.

"Cian!" Jack shouted once more.

"Up the corridor more, my lord," the publican told him, his voice soft.

Time had run out.

Cian gripped the curtain once more.

"They've scheduled my wedding," Eleanore said.

Each word was a nail into his heart. Cian hung his head. "When?" His lips wouldn't work properly.

"May next year."

"So soon…" He sighed. "You're leaving for Skye even sooner."

"At the end of the month. Passage has already been booked on the *Highland Queen*. My father is anxious to go fishing with the laird."

"Letters from there will be uncertain…" He grimaced. "The world is separating us whether we wish it or no."

She pressed her hand over her heart. "The world cannot reach here."

The curtain was flung aside. "There you are," Jack said, peeved. "What on earth did you think you were doing, jumping on a runaway carriage, Cian? You could have been killed. Then your mother would have killed *me*."

Eleanore's gaze didn't leave Cian's face.

Cian took a deep breath for courage, then turned to face Jack and the world that would not let them be.

Chapter Six

In the last year, Bronwen had learned from observation that running a very large estate was not a simple matter. Jasper left early in the morning and was often gone for most of the day, inspecting properties, coordinating laborers, settling tenant disputes, complaints and more.

Even Lilly had been drawn into taking care of administrative responsibilities, although she did not tour with Jasper. Instead, she remained at the desk that had been installed in her morning room, dealing with correspondence and documents that Jasper simply did not have time to manage.

Jasper could hire an estate manager to take over both his and Lilly's work and live the life of a gentleman, instead. It was how things were normally done. Bronwen had asked Jasper why he did not follow the custom, when the work was so onerous. His answer had been frank.

"This estate has been mired in local feuds for generations precisely because the owner was absent and the management left it in indifferent hands. These Yorkshire men have begun to trust me." He grimaced. "It has only taken five years," he added. "They like knowing they're speaking to the man who makes the real decisions. They like that their complaints are heard and fairly addressed. If I thrust an estate manager at them, they will feel as though I am throwing their trust back at them. I would never regain the ground I would lose."

Therefore, Jasper and Lilly continued to labor over the estate, putting their hearts and souls into the betterment of the land for the sake of the farmers whose lives and families depended upon their good management.

Because the pair were busy during the day, Bronwen was rarely interrupted when she spent the day in the library. She could sit where and how she pleased, read any book she wanted and be perfectly happy doing it.

The Northallerton library was no ordinary family library. It far outstripped her own family's libraries, which were large, inclusive collections. Her parents' library was considered to be the largest private library in London, with exceedingly rare documents that experts and scholars sometimes begged to study. Her parents liked to read widely. Bronwen could remember family meals where the only topic of conversation was a single point of logic or reason in a book they had read.

When Bronwen was twelve, she had found Sadie in the library after one loudly debated supper, bent over the book in question.

"You're reading it, too?" Bronwen asked, astonished.

Sadie tossed her thick blonde braid over her shoulder and pinned Bronwen with her blue eyes. "I want to understand what Mother and Father were arguing about. Don't you?"

"I suppose, yes," Bronwen said. "Only, they were talking about sub...sub-you..."

"Subjugation," Sadie replied. "Slavery, in all its many

forms."

"Isn't that a subject for adults?" Bronwen asked, creeping closer to the book. Sadie was only three years older than her.

"Why must it be only for adults?" Sadie demanded.

Bronwen couldn't find an answer. "It just seems... complicated." There had been ideas and thoughts raised at dinner that had baffled her. That was not unusual, though. Not in the Davies household.

"Because you didn't read the book," Sadie said.

"Oh..." Bronwen leaned over the open book and looked at the script. "That's why you're reading it? Because you didn't understand?"

There was a flash of something in Sadie's eyes. Then the corner of her mouth turned up. "I don't like not knowing things."

"Is that what they were talking about? That page you're on?" Bronwen asked.

"The entire chapter," Sadie corrected, turning back the pages to the beginning. Both of them read.

Twenty minutes later, Rhys stepped into the library and paused at the door when he saw them both at the reading stand.

Bronwen drew back, guilt spearing her.

Her father crossed the room and picked up the whisky decanter and a glass. "Don't smear the pages," he said, his tone light. "There was treacle for desert and neither of you knows how to eat without using your fingers."

That was the first time Bronwen had found answers to

something that had puzzled her within the covers of a book. Because her family's library was so extensive, over the years she had found many more answers there. Most of them were far more explicit and on-point than the vague responses of her governess, who believed young ladies needed to know French, embroidery, protocol and regimental insignia and nothing else.

Books had become Bronwen's tools for negotiating the adult world.

The library at Northallerton, though, was an idyllic escape. The estate had been established shortly after the English Civil War and various owners had been collecting books and manuscripts, treatises and literature, ever since. There were musty old hand-lettered volumes in the back shelves of the library that Bronwen suspected had not been read since the estate acquired them. The middle English had been a challenge to read, although Bronwen had swiftly learned to read it with the same ease she read modern English.

The library was a huge room that rose through both floors of the house. A gallery ran around all four walls, with shelves climbing to the ceiling and ladders to reach the highest of them.

There were reading desks, tables, comfortable chairs and lamps to ease the readers' sojourn. Instead, Bronwen most often stood where she had discovered the current book. It was easier to sit where she was. Usually, upon the step ladder. Then the reshelving was a simple matter.

The Northallerton library was a treasure trove, although the secret core of that treasure was the extended collection of medical texts.

Somewhere in Northallerton's history, an owner had been a doctor or interested in medicine. The rare compendiums, folios and monographs dealt with the most obscure medical knowledge. It was a folded leaflet tucked among those pages that had raised the theory that dock plants salved nettle stings because of the acid/base relationship.

Agatha was a font of herbal lore and medicinal cures, yet her learning had been handed from mother to daughter, the science behind the knowledge absent. In the last year, Bronwen had learned many of the real explanations here in Jasper's library.

When the door to the library opened barely an hour after she had settled with a book, Bronwen looked up, surprised. She was rarely disturbed here. Even Warrick had learned she did not care for tea and refreshments when she was reading.

Tor stepped through the door, looking around with a surprised expression.

Bronwen's heart sank. She had forgotten for a while that the man was in the house. Now he had broken her peace.

Tor spotted her sitting on the stairs leading up to the gallery. "Ah…" He shut the door and moved into the room, threading through a pair of leather armchairs. "A riddle is answered."

"The riddle being 'how can I best interrupt Bronwen?'" she asked, closing the book with a thud.

His gaze met hers. There was no rancor there. Given how rude she had been to him the previous evening, the lack of animosity was a surprise. "The riddle was, 'where did she learn about biological chemicals, when students of the Sorbonne must study for years to be granted access to such tomes?'"

"I *have* studied for years."

He turned on his heel, taking in every inch of the large room. "I believe you."

"I suppose you're one of those people who thinks women have no need of higher education?"

"I suppose you're one of those women who intends to study at the new ladies' college at Cambridge, when it opens?"

"Where I am told what I must read?" Bronwen shook her head. "They will not issue degrees to women even if they pass their examinations with higher marks than the men. Why would I bother with Cambridge when there is more knowledge here on these shelves?"

Tor glanced about the room once more. He was dressed this morning in a dark frock coat and striped cravat. The cravat was pinned crookedly.

Was this the first time he had ever pinned a cravat himself? Bronwen suspected that there were many tasks he must undertake that he had never done before.

What would make a man like him suffer through the many petty irritations such a lack of experience would bring him? Why run away?

His gaze came back to her. He glanced at the closed book on her knees. "I should leave you to your reading."

"Yes."

Yet, he did not move.

Bronwen sighed and rested her forearms on the book and linked her fingers together, waiting.

Tor came closer to the stairs. "I feel I should apologize for last evening."

"I accept your apology. Now…" She lifted the book.

He stopped at the foot of the stairs. She was sitting on the fifth step, which put her head at his level. "We got off to a bad start," he said.

Bronwen shook her head. "We are not at the start of anything. You are a temporary guest in the house where I live and that is all. How we interact while you are here has no bearing on the long term. Be rude if you must. It is immaterial to me."

He examined her for a long, silent moment. Bronwen did not writhe under his gaze. Why should she? She felt no guilt for her plain speaking. She had been honest. It was not her fault if he found the truth unpalatable.

"There is not a single curse in your speech," he said, "yet I feel insulted. I cannot fathom why."

Bronwen linked her fingers together once more. "You feel insulted because I am utterly indifferent about you. I imagine indifference is a novelty to a man like you."

His gaze turned inward. "Yes, I suspect you are right. I have never met someone who cares so little about me."

"No?" she asked, her tone cool. "Or do they merely let you think they care?"

"Disingenuity *is* a blight of the higher ranked life," he admitted. He put his foot on the first step and bent closer.

"*Why* do you not care?"

Bronwen straightened up, putting distance between them. "Why do you care why I don't care?"

"I am curious."

"You seek more insults? One is not enough?"

"There is a violence to your indifference…it is as though you are protesting too much. Shakespeare had that right."

"'The lady doth protest too much, methinks,'" Bronwen quoted.

"'O, but she'll keep her word,'" Tor replied, which was the next line. His smile was small. "Shakespeare's Prince of Denmark has lessons for everyone," he added.

"You *like* that I insult you every time we speak?"

"We have only spoken twice," he pointed out, for he had been absent at the breakfast table. "This moment is that second occasion. You have been honest, both times. Honest and direct."

"Ah." She put her hands on the book, resting them there. "It is true, I am forcing myself to remain indifferent about you. The world you live in, who you really are…these are things far outside my own small life. You have descended upon Jasper's house, using your connection to buy yourself an adventure. Then, when you have taken your fill, you will return to your life, never to look down upon us again." She shrugged. "Therefore, I will remain indifferent to you. You will soon be gone."

Tor straightened with a snap, as if she had slapped him. His eyes narrowed. "You think I am looking for a toy to play with. The distraction of novelty, to appease my *ennui*."

"I cannot imagine anyone running from the life of privilege you enjoy for any other reason."

He spun away, as if emotions were driving his feet. He walked in a tight, hard circle and came back to the stair. His jaw was tight.

Bronwen felt no fear, despite the clear signs of anger he displayed. He would not dare touch her. If he tried, she was sitting at just the right height to kick him and today, she wore her boots, too.

His hands gripped the iron railings. The knuckles whitened. "You know *nothing* of my life."

"Precisely."

He shook his head. "You read these books, yet you fail to absorb their lessons." He swallowed, his jaw working. "Have you studied the symptoms and treatment of cholera?"

"Briefly." Her heart gave a little squeeze.

"Have you ever *seen* a cholera victim?" He shook his head. "Don't bother answering. I know you have not. You are a maiden, living a sheltered and indulged life. You have wisdom of a kind from your reading, while you have no real experience of life."

"And you have?" She tried to laugh. It sounded strained.

"I visited the hospital in Edinburgh," he said, his voice low. "*Every* day for a week, to see if there was anything I or my people could do." His gaze turned inward. "The stench turns your stomach. Then there are the moans and screams of pain. People collapse in on themselves, turning into dried out husks, in a matter of hours."

"Dehydration…" Bronwen whispered.

"They contort themselves and scream while they are doing it," he added. "The children are the worst. They thrash on their pallets and their eyes roll." His gaze came back to her face. "Death is a relief, after that."

Bronwen swallowed, her heart thudding.

"I watched people suffer and knew there was nothing I could do about it and not just because this is not my country or my people." He pushed himself off the stairs with a hard thrust and turned away. "My own country suffers," he added, his voice low. "There is a sickness that has gripped it for years. People die. Healthy, young people. Old, frail people. Women, children, men. The sickness does not distinguish who it chooses as its next victim. It can strike anyone and every time the symptoms are different. No expert can tell me what is the cause." He turned to face her. His throat worked. "And they look to *me* to provide answers, to fix everything for them. I am their overlord. It is my duty to protect them and I am failing."

Bronwen didn't dare move, for the impotent fury radiated from him in waves. His hands were fisted by his sides. The tension in his shoulders made him look like a man on the verge of exploding.

Then he drew in a heavy, harsh breath. And another. His shoulders settled and he flexed his hands.

"I do not linger here looking for an adventure," he added, his tone dry.

"You think you will find answers here? In the Yorkshire dales?" She couldn't prevent the note of incredulity in her voice.

He ruffled his hair with a rough movement, as if he were trying to scrub away his frustration. "If I seek anything at all, it is the hope that I might find...perspective." There was bitterness in his eyes. "Of course, someone as indifferent as you would not care to understand that, either."

He moved away, his steps fused with the anger he had subsumed.

"Socrates said a change of context can promote critical thinking," Bronwen said.

He turned to look at her. His brow lifted. "Exactly." He sounded surprised.

Bronwen put the book on the step, got to her feet and moved to the floor. "I was wrong about you," she admitted. "I thought that...well, you know what I thought. I misunderstood. I am sorry."

He studied her for a moment, then let out a rushed breath. "You have an uncommon clarity of self. Most men are incapable of seeing their mistakes even when presented with evidence. Even more are incapable of admitting it."

Bronwen shrugged. "I am not a man."

He smiled. "Perhaps I was wrong about you, too."

"Most people misunderstand me. That is not a difficult admission to make."

He nodded. "Your indifference *makes* them misinterpret. I assumed you were merely a woman grasping for freedom in any way she could and to Hades with societal expectations. Only, you are *using* your freedom." He lifted his hand and waved it to take in the room. "For this. Freedom gives you the means to study and not in some controlled college with narrow-minded professors."

Bronwen couldn't help smiling. Her pleasure warmed her. Few people grasped so quickly why she lived the way she did.

Tor sat on the arm of the sofa and crossed his arms. "What have you studied? Where has your reading taken you?"

Her surprise made her start. "You really wish to know?"

"Yes."

Bronwen recalled the many facets of human knowledge she had tapped, some deeply and some of which she had only skated the surface. "I take knowledge wherever it is available," she said, as a different idea occurred to her. "Tell me, are you really looking for a fresh perspective to jolt you into new ways of thinking?"

Tor frowned. "A succinct way of putting it. Yes, that is what I seek, although until your indifference pushed me into describing it, I did not know it."

Bronwen nodded. "Then you must come with me."

His arms dropped. "Where?"

"Wherever I go. Come and see for yourself what I see and observe. Today, I want to visit Agatha and make sure her cottage survived the rainstorm and help her hang the rosemary for drying."

"Should I call for the carriage?"

"Don't be silly. We'll walk."

"Walk," he repeated, sounding flummoxed.

"Do you even own a pair of boots?" she asked, eyeing

his elegant shoes.

"Perhaps Jasper will lend me a pair."

"Hop to it, then," Bronwen told him. "It's five miles to Agatha's and I would prefer to be home for lunch. Cook has made cottage pie."

Tor looked affronted. "Hop to it?" He raised his brow.

"You're not a prince of Denmark here, remember?" She met his gaze. "Perspective," she reminded him.

"Yes," he agreed and strode to the door.

Bronwen went to collect her shawl and bonnet, resisting the warm trickle of appreciation that a man had listened to her—*actually* listened—and no lesser man than the Archeduke Edvard Christoffer, at that.

For her, he should remain merely Tor Besogende, too.

Chapter Seven

Sometimes, in the morning, Rhys found it difficult to get his hands to work as they should. At first, it had been a mere stiffness that had soon worked itself out as the day passed. Lately, though, especially on cold mornings such as this one, his fingers would not cooperate.

It was not the first unsettling sign of aging he had noticed, only the most severe one. Usually, he ignored that he was fifty-five years old, because he still felt like a young man. At least, he did if he avoided mirrors. The gray in his hair was always a shock to him.

Instead of telling Anna he could not manage his cravat for himself as he had his entire life, he announced he would not go to the office today. Anna would fuss and worry if he said why. Instead, he spoke of a light schedule and Benjamin's more than competent handling of the partners.

Rhys slid his dressing gown over his shirt and made his way downstairs, flexing and cracking his knuckles, trying to restore feeling to his fingers. He would settle in the library and read the newspapers—all of them—from front page to back. Then there was that excellent new volume by John Stuart Mill on the reading stand…

Alice was sitting at the desk, writing. She looked up when Rhys entered and smiled, her green eyes dancing and her dimples deepening. "I hope you don't mind, Father? Your desk is much nicer for writing than the dining room."

She was a pretty sight, in an apple green dress and a white ribbon trailing from the back of her hair. She looked fresh and lovely and sweet.

"I don't mind at all," Rhys assured her. He enjoyed the way the morning sun was make her pale blonde hair gleam. Her skin was clear and so pale it sometimes seemed it might be transparent. "You don't like the morning room?"

Alice wrinkled her nose. "Iefan has been smoking in there. The smoke makes me cough until it hurts."

"That was last night, wasn't it?" Rhys asked, for Iefan had left for Sussex on the morning train to follow up with clients.

"It still makes me cough."

"Then you are welcome to use my desk. Who are you writing to?"

"Neil." Alice's cheeks bloomed red. She concentrated on the blotting of her pen. Her breathing quickened.

Rhys made himself sort through the folded newspapers just as he had been, while his mind raced. "Neil is in Northumberland now?"

"His regiment returned to barracks last month."

"How did the India campaign go?"

"There was no battles at all. Just heat and dust and elephants. Neil was very disappointed."

Then Neil was writing back to her and sharing intimate details. Rhys wondered if Vaughn and Elisa were aware of the correspondence, although he didn't for a moment wonder if they approved of their son's alliance with his daughter. Neil had grown into a fine man and an even better officer.

Rhys cleared his throat. "Has he...spoken to you, Alice?"

Alice lifted her gaze to meet his. Her face was flushed. "He wanted to come to the Gathering, Father, only the boat was delayed. He has leave at Christmas and he said he would try to make it to London..." She bit her lip. "I'm sure he will speak to me then." Her gaze dropped to her hands, as if she had run out of courage.

Rhys lifted her chin, to make her look at him. "Do you love him, darling daughter?"

Her eyes glowed. *She* glowed. "I do."

"Then no matter when he speaks to you, it will be time enough. Neil is a good man. He won't make you wait."

Her happiness welled up inside her, turning her expression into one of pure joy.

Rhys hugged her. He couldn't help it. Her simple pleasure and love were infectious.

"Oh, Daddy, I'm so happy!" she whispered, her cheek against his shoulder. "I don't know why Sadie and Bronwen insist upon finding happiness somewhere out in the world when it is right here inside me!"

"They're just not as lucky as you, my sweet one," Rhys told her. Fierce love overwhelmed him, making his vision blur and his heart to throb. Of his four daughters, Alice was the sweet one, the quiet one, the one he had been afraid would be lost behind the strident clamoring of the others.

Neil had seen her beauty and goodness, though. Thank God for that.

Rhys kissed her silky hair, relief making him dizzy.

Alice coughed and leaned away from him. She waved her hand in front of her face and coughed again. "Goodness, Father. Your gown reeks of smoke!"

"I don't smoke," Rhys pointed out.

"Wood smoke!" She coughed again. The sound was a harsh bark that pulled from the depths of her lungs. It hurt to hear it. Rhys hid his grimace as Alice got herself back under control.

She rolled her eyes. "I'm sorry." She pressed her hand to her mouth, covering it as she gave another small cough. "The tiniest whiff of smoke sets me off." She dropped her hand and smiled an apology at him.

Rhys caught her hand and lifted it up so he could see clearly.

There were red spots sprayed across the palm.

His heart turned to ice.

"What is it, Father?" Alice asked.

Hiding his reaction, he reached into his pocket and withdrew his handkerchief and cleaned off her palm. "It's nothing," he lied. "Nothing at all. Finish your letter to Neil, my darling. Enjoy yourself."

Her face lit. "I will." She picked up the pen, eager to return to the letter.

Rhys made himself walk away, struggling to look normal as he did, for now, not just his hands wouldn't cooperate. Everything had seized up, except for his heart, which careened about like a wild bird in a cage.

* * * * *

Bronwen looked up from the page she was reading, putting together Price's Theorem of Reason in her head.

Her gaze took in the entire library, because she was sitting at the top of the stairs, up by where the book had been shelved.

Tor was in the armchair, which was pulled up to the fire, for it was a blustery, wet day. He was sitting, more or less. She had shown him how to arrange himself so his legs supported heavy books. It involved draping the knees over the armchair and propping the book against one's legs, which held it open. Leaning back against the other arm put just the right distance between the book and the eyes.

It was the ideal posture for reading for hours at a time, only most people objected to the lounging sprawl. Tor had taken to it with speed.

He was wearing Jasper's walking clothes. The rough tweed jacket and pants were made for walking about the vale and through trees. The shirt had no collar and was open at the neck, revealing pale flesh beneath that was nevertheless dipped in the center between the musculature. Bronwen had studied anatomy books and knew of the chest muscles that made the flesh pillow in that way. It was fascinating to see it in a live subject, though.

The shirt was too small across the shoulders and pulled the fabric taut over Tor's chest in an agreeable way.

How much he had changed in four days!

Bronwen recalled the way he'd sat on the arm of that very chair, the first day he had stepped in the library. The upright carriage and the stiff formality. He'd perched, not sat. Even his feet had been together.

Now his hair was tousled, his clothing that of a workman. He had cultivated a new perspective with systematic thoroughness. At times, he had forced himself to overcome habits of thought and practice that would prevent him from thoroughly experiencing everything.

His relentless mowing down and raking aside of old attitudes and testing new ones had been fascinating to watch. She had never met anyone with such discipline.

Tor lifted his hand to turn the page. His wrist, the one she had turned to examine nettle stings, showed the flex of strong tendons beneath as the long fingers eased the page over.

A stray thought leapt into her mind. What would it feel like to have that hand, those long fingers, against her? Right there, against her chest, above the top of her camisole, which he would feel through the cotton of her dress....

Bronwen dropped her gaze back to her book as confusion swamped her. Her cheeks burned.

She didn't...she couldn't...desire him, could she?

Remember who he really is, she whispered in her mind.

It didn't matter that he wasn't really Tor Besogende. It didn't matter that his changed appearance was an attempt by him to jolt himself into finding a way forward into the future.

What did matter was the determined way he was going about it.

And that he was a man, just like any other. Hot blooded. Flesh and bone.

Only, she couldn't want him. It was impossible. She had never desired a man. Ever. Most of them she found to be tiresome and shallow, far too in love with their own selves to consider loving another. Or they were simply too stupid to withstand more than a few moments in their company.

The text on the page she was staring at was a reminder. *Reason deductively*, she told herself.

Tor was a man. She was a woman. They were healthy people. They were spending time in each other's company. Wouldn't it be more surprising if she was unmoved by him at all?

Except...except...oh, he was the very last man she should feel anything for!

Bronwen realized she was studying him once more. Her gaze followed the long line of his legs over the armchair and down to the flat plane of his stomach where the edge of the book rested. She took in the tight fabric of the shirt stretched across his chest and the flesh beneath it.

She had long ago educated herself on the mysteries of sex and copulation. This was the first time, though, she had stared at a man's crotch and wondered about the appearance of what lay beneath the buttons of his trousers.

She was growing breathless simply speculating.

"Damn," she whispered to herself, borrowing Sadie's favorite curse.

"Did you say something?" Tor asked, looking up at where she sat.

She had not spoken as softly as she thought. Bronwen cast about for an answer. "I was...arguing to myself the points of Mr. Price's theory on the superiority of deductive reasoning over inductive reasoning."

Tor frowned. "Deductive reasoning..." He sat up, bringing his feet to the floor, so he was facing her. "That is where I say: All men have beards. My father has a beard. Therefore my father is a man. Yes?"

"Only, not all men have beards," Bronwen pointed out. "The base assumption is incorrect. If your base assumptions are correct, then your conclusion *must* be correct. That is why Mr. Price considers deductive reasoning superior."

"Inductive reasoning can still be wrong even if the data is correct?" Tor smiled. "It certainly sounds as though inductive reasoning is the weaker of the two."

"Simplistic drivel," Bronwen said, putting the offending book aside. "It is as if Mr. Price has never read Sir Isaac Newton, or Rene Descartes. He ignores the rationality of inductive reasoning, how it allows rigorous testing in search of the truth. Yes, the hypothesis may be wrong, only testing will prove it wrong. Deductive reasoning does not allow testing or the discovery of errors and that makes deductive reasoning the weaker of the two."

Tor closed his own book. "That is why you swear?" His deep blue eyes caught hers.

Bronwen got to her feet and climbed to the main floor and swept past him. "I'm hungry. It must be near afternoon tea. Coming?"

Tor considered her for a moment. Then he put the book down and followed.

* * * * *

"Will you be heading out this afternoon, Bronwen?" Lilly asked, as she put down the teapot. "It is a mild day, perhaps one of the last this year."

Bronwen frowned. She had intended to stay in the library all day. Now, though, the idea of staying indoors was intolerable. She grasped the straw that Lilly had provided. "Yes," she said firmly. "A short walk, to clear the cobwebs."

"Will you be accompanying her, Tor?" Lilly asked.

Tor put down the slice of fruitcake he had been eating. "I would not presume to intrude upon Bronwen's excursion without her permission. I know how much she likes her solitude."

Relief trickled through her. Bronwen tried to look apologetic. "I would prefer to wander alone, thank you. Besides, you are still to finish Mr. Darwin."

"*The Origins of Species*?" Lilly clarified. "How do you find Darwin, Tor? Do you consider him to be the blasphemous fool the newspapers call him?"

Tor smiled. "I can understand why many think that of him. It is uncomfortable to entertain the idea that humans are descendants of monkeys, with no higher purpose than the apes. Although I have been reminded that reason is a tool for reaching the truth. If I use that tool, then I must say that Charles Darwin makes rational sense. Whether I like that sense is immaterial."

"Hmm…" Lilly said, fixing him with a look from under her brow. "You sound just like Bronwen."

"Truth is truth," Tor said, with a tiny shrug of one shoulder.

Bronwen caught his glance toward her and tried to ignore the skip and leap of her heart.

Truth was a sharp tool. The truth was, she could not afford to be drawn to this man in any way. A walk out in the dales, with the wind whipping her hair and chilling her face and hands, was just what she needed.

* * * * *

Once Lilly had returned to her immeasurable duties and Bronwen had departed upon her short walk, Tor returned to the library. He glanced at the big portfolio sized volume of Darwin, lying waiting for him.

Mr. Darwin had lost all appeal.

Instead, Tor wandered the library, sliding his fingertip across the spines of volumes, absorbing the titles and the boundless range of topics and subjects. A restless energy gripped him.

As he took another turn about the library, he grew aware of the throbbing pain building in his head. Now his inability to settle to reading was explained. He paused at the far end of the big library, looking up at the dust motes dancing in the sunlight shining through the windows.

He should return to his borrowed room before the pain grew stronger. He was familiar with these attacks and knew the course this one would take.

Only, why was he being inflicted with the malady today?

No one knew of the debilitating headaches. At least, no one in his dukedom knew. There was a certain German doctor, Heinzman, whom Tor had contrived to have visit him in secret, a year ago. The man was an expert in matters of the head and the brain, yet his consultation had been useless.

"A relaxation of the mind and the soul, no?" Heinzman said, pressing his hands together. "Less work and more pleasure, that is the answer. You know what they say about all work and no play."

Tor had paid the doctor and sent him on his way, disappointed by the useless diagnosis.

The headaches had persisted. Not many—certainly not enough of them to lead anyone to suspect him of ill-health, which would put Baumgärtner, the Council and the entire dukedom into a panic. Silkeborg most certainly did not need such uncertainty these days.

Tor did not have time to be ill, yet the headaches would ensure an entire day was wasted while he lingered behind a locked door and prayed he would not be called upon to tend to an emergency and be revealed to the world.

If the doctor, Heinzman, had been correct and it was simply a matter of less taxing work, then why was a headache visiting Tor here, in Northallerton, the most peaceful location in which he'd ever lingered?

Tor made his way toward the door, moving with deliberate slowness as he considered the puzzle.

Only, with every step toward the exit, his headache bloomed larger and stronger, until he could think of nothing but the exquisite pain. His vision blurred.

Feeling blindly ahead, he turned and moved toward the sofa, instead. He would not be able to negotiate the stairs and the route to his room. Not now.

He lay on the sofa and gripped his head. His fingers added to the agony. Breathing in soft, shallow sips, he waited. He had waited in this way many times in the past. His thoughts fell into a darkness, unnoticed, as the pain moved to the forefront of his consciousness.

Time had no meaning. He only realized the short afternoon was growing to a close when the lowering sun burst through the high window up by the ceiling and dazzled him where he lay on the sofa, immobile.

He winced, despite his closed eyes.

"Tor, what is wrong?" Bronwen asked, from nearby.

Then her shadow fell across his face, blocking the light that danced redly against his eye lids.

Tor eased open one eye. "Nothing," he said, the lie coming to him automatically. He shut his eye again,

"Nothing is making you wince in that way and hiss with pain?"

He heard the soft rustle of her hems.

"You have a headache?" she asked, from much closer.

Tor opened his eye once more. "A headache is far too limiting a description for this."

Bronwen had lowered herself next to the sofa to examine him. She tilted her head. Her large gray eyes considered him. "I have read of such headaches before. Stay there…" She grimaced. "Of course you will stay there. I will be but a moment. I have something I suspect will help." She rose to her feet.

"Shut the door," he whispered and closed his eyes once more, surrendering to the throbbing.

He didn't hear her leave. He didn't hear her return. The first notice he received that she was back was the touch of her cool fingers against his wrist. "Put your arm down. I must reach your temples."

Tor eased his arm away from shielding his eyes, returning it to his side. The movement sent a roll of agony through him and he held still, waiting for the thunder in his mind to ease.

Her fingertips were pressing against his head. Soft touches on either side, then the center of his forehead.

Another touch under the back of his neck.

Where her fingers had touched, cool liquid eased the skin there. It was like the touch of water on a hot day.

"Let yourself sample the aroma," she told him. "It is very pleasant."

He could smell it now. It was distinct and unique. "Lavender," he whispered.

"Oil of lavender," she replied. "An old wife told me how to ease headaches." He heard the humor in her voice.

Only, he was not in the mood to jest. He still did not dare open his eyes wide. "A dab of oil against the flesh is hardly scientific."

"Wait and see," Bronwen assured him.

As he could do little more than wait, he was forced to obey her instructions. He let his eyes shut once more and wondered how he could ensure Bronwen remained silent about his temporary condition.

He could hear her moving about the big room not because she tramped heavily, but because the room was so silent the swish of her hems against the floor gave her movements away.

Then, the soft sound of pages being turned. She was reading.

Time passed. Tor resigned himself to spending the long hours the headache would continue here upon this sofa. He would have to negotiate with Bronwen later, to secure her discretion.

The change was so gradual that at first, Tor did not realize the headache was lessening. His first hint was when his head did not throb and threaten to explode when he shifted too quickly upon the leather.

He deliberately turned his head again, rolling it to one side.

Yes, the sickening, swooping bellow of pain was gone. His head thudded. It was a minor ache, somewhat similar to what he suffered in the morning after a heavy night of cards, drinking and smoking. That pain was easily tolerated.

Carefully, he opened his eyes.

He could see without his stomach roiling.

Intense relief circled through him. The worst of the headache had disappeared. Her oil of lavender had worked.

Tor pushed himself up until he could put his back against the padded arm of the sofa.

Bronwen stepped around the reading stand and came to him, her smile soft and warm. "It worked, then." She lowered herself to meet his eyes once more, her gaze traveling over his face, assessing.

"It appears it has," Tor said. "Perhaps learning why should be your next research project. It really is simple oil of lavender you used?"

"It really is simple oil of lavender." She slid her hand into her pocket and withdrew a small, dark brown glass bottle with a waxed stopper and a hand-written label. "I made the extract myself, although any competent herbalist could do the same." She held the bottle out to him. "You should take this."

He met her gaze. "I will have no future need of it," he lied.

Bronwen's smile was tiny. "I have been reading, while waiting for the lavender to work. Most people consider headaches to be a woman's complaint and men who suffer them to be malingerers reaching for an excuse to escape their duties. Only, a Flemish doctor—Aarden—pointed out that the very worst of the headaches, the ones that leave a person prostrate, come most often to the opposite type of person. The person who does not cease, who considers leisure to be unholy sloth." Her gaze met his. "This is not the first time you have had such a headache, is it?"

Tor drew in a breath, startled. "You have given exactly the same diagnosis the most expensive expert in Europe supplied."

Bronwen held out the small bottle once more. "Take it," she said. "You will have need of it in the future. Your palace cannot be anywhere near as calm as Northallerton."

He took the bottle, considering her. "I don't suppose your reading has told you why I fell victim to this onslaught, here in placid Northallerton?"

Bronwen's smile was rueful. "Perhaps the lack of calm is here," she said, her fingers resting briefly against his temple. "Only you know what is in your thoughts."

Her touch was soft. It brought her wrist close enough for him to register the warmth against his cheek. Her scent was intriguing. Unlike the usual rose water or one of the flowery alternatives sophisticated women favored, he sampled the most delicate mix of spices. He could name none of them. His heart beat harder. It was as though he recognized the scent, even though he knew he had never come across it before.

He closed his eyes, wishing the scent would linger awhile, for it was so pleasant. His heart hurried on even harder, while at the base of his belly, tension curled.

"Did you just sniff my wrist?" Bronwen asked. Her voice was strained.

Tor looked at her. She cradled her hand as if he had injured it. "You should not wear such a scent if the sniffing of it gives you offense."

She lowered her wrist. "I wear no scent. If I did, the strength of the oil of lavender would mask it."

Tor stared at her, at last recognizing the strain in his body for what it was. He wanted her—this plain, strange woman who challenged him at every turn. It was not a voluntary decision. His body had arrived at the conclusion independently of his mind. It had not occurred to him to even entertain the possibility of Bronwen as a potential dalliance. That was not why he was here.

Such matters were possible, yet complicated. They took careful negotiation and arrangements that involved discrete conversations and the assistance of Baumgärtner and his most trusted employees. A night in a country inn, away from the eyes of his people. A "chance" encounter in a country where neither of them would be recognized... Tor had risked such affairs a few times since his father had died, although they were time-consuming, perilous adventures. The ladies he considered worthy of such effort were self-contained, highly cultured women who understood the politics. Adventuresses themselves, they knew the value of discretion.

Bronwen was not that sort of woman. She was not any type of woman. She was unique.

And inaccessible. She was a distant cousin by marriage, a young woman of royal descent, marriageable and, he presumed, innocent. She was Jasper's guest, just as he was. Tor would not despoil his brother's guest under Jasper's roof. It would be an insult to Jasper and a larger insult to Bronwen, too, for there could be no permanent outcome to such an affair.

The impossibility of indulging in his physical interest in her passed through Tor's mind in the brief moment their eyes met, as his body tightened and his heart squeezed.

He should return to his room and put the stout door between him and temptation. Instead, he remained where he was, his body throbbing in a different, far more pleasurable way.

He might have stayed there until he gathered the will to get to his feet and leave the room as he must. Only, Bronwen swayed forward. Her lips met his.

Tor was too shocked to move. Never in his life had a woman dared to initiate such an intimacy. He was the Archeduke. It was he who chose whom he kissed and when.

The intoxicating scent washed over him, making his skin prickle and his belly to tighten even more.

Then her tongue slid against his lips. The soft heat of it acted as a goad, triggering him into unthinking reaction. He pulled her against him, bringing her over his chest so he could kiss her deeply. He held her face, reveling in the smooth delicate silk of her skin under his fingers. She had a small face, which surprised him because she seemed much larger in his mind.

Then he realized what he was doing and to whom. His mind stirred. The protest, the alarm, was faint. Reluctant. It was enough for sanity to restore itself, though.

Tor didn't push her away. He couldn't bring himself to do that. He lifted his mouth from hers.

Bronwen breathed heavily, her lips swollen and red. Her eyes, the gray pure and rich, were warm with…

Tor shook his head. "We cannot."

"Why not?"

Tor's breath expelled heavily as he cast about for a simple answer. "I am…me. You are my brother's family."

Bronwen lifted herself off him. She had been lying against his chest, which told him how much the moment of insanity had stolen his good sense. With her weight gone, cool air rushed in to replace her heat. He shivered in reaction, which was yet another measure of the tight heat in his body.

She settled on the floor, her hands in her lap. Her gaze was unflinching. There was no shame in her. No upset at his rejection. "You are Tor Besogende. What of that man prevents anything?"

Tor sat up and pushed his hand through his hair. "Besogende is just a name, something for other people to grasp, that allows me to stay here without complications. It isn't me." He stopped himself from finishing the thought aloud.

It wasn't Tor Besogende who had kissed her.

"Besides," he added, his voice rough, "you are a lady of good family. Such a lady—"

"You are about to lecture me on morals?" she asked, her voice rising. "After everything you have read and heard me say this past week?"

Tor hesitated.

Bronwen got to her feet. "Have you not learned that I care nothing for the artificial concepts of morals and etiquette? Only the truth interests me. The truth I can see for myself in your eyes. I can see it in the way your chest rises."

Tor pressed his hand against his betraying chest. "You do not understand. Nothing could come of...of following our impulses. No matter how truthful they are."

Her gaze met his. Her chin came up. "I expected nothing but a pleasant experience."

Tor clenched his hands together. "You *should* have," he said flatly. "You are worthy of far higher expectations than you allow yourself."

Her expression softened. "Thank you." She got to her feet and brushed out the folds of her dress.

Tor automatically rose to his feet, the habit ingrained. The movement did not jar his head or start it throbbing. Even the mild ache was leaving.

Bronwen's gaze met his once more. There was no coyness there. "I *do* know who I am and my expectations. You are the confused one. That is why you came here, is it not? In search of perspective?"

"I would not sully you merely to achieve it."

Bronwen laughed and moved toward the door.

Tor spun to watch her leave. "Why do you laugh?"

Bronwen opened the door and stepped through, then turned to put her hand on the outside handle. She drew the door halfway closed and looked at him. "You do not earn the privilege of my favor without it."

She shut the door.

Startled, Tor sank back onto the sofa. He was still sitting there when dinner was announced, forcing him to hurry to his room and change.

His evening clothes smelled dry, the starch caustic, making him think of state dinners, braid and tiaras, sashes and medals. He heard the slap of ceremonial swords against legs. Danish spoken softly, the French of diplomats spoken badly. Decorative women who did not speak until spoken to.

It was a relief to step out into the wide corridor and

move downstairs to where the warm fire crackled and children with piping voices sat at the table with the adults, where everyone spoke freely, including Bronwen.

Chapter Eight

Bronwen eased open the door of her room and winced at the squeak of the hinges. She had not consciously noticed the small sound the door made, until now.

Moonlight bathed the hall runner, making the patterns of white glow among the reds and blacks. Bronwen stepped onto the carpet, which muffled her footsteps, grateful that Lilly followed the European custom of laying rugs even in little used areas such as corridors and hallways. It was an exorbitant practice, although it kept Bronwen's bare feet off the cold floor.

Her heart pattering, Bronwen eased along the corridor toward the door at the far end, listening to the silence in the big house.

Did she intend to go through with this? The question rose in her mind, as if spoken by another. She fancied she could hear another woman's voice asking it. It was not her mother's voice, for Bronwen suspected her mother would only warn her to reduce the risk in her decision in any way she could. The voice she thought she could hear was Elisa's. Or perhaps, Natasha's. Except both women had taken equally bold risks when they were younger.

As she moved down the dim corridor, Bronwen re-examined her reasoning one last time.

Tor had not said he didn't want her. He had said he could not—*would* not—indulge himself when there was no future in it.

Only, Bronwen had caught him watching her through-out dinner. His contributions to the conversation had been sparse and absent-minded. His gaze had been heated.

Bronwen excused herself immediately after the meal. She escaped, not to the library where he would find her, but to the sanctuary of her room where she could think in peace.

Only there, Tor's absence drove home a relevant fact she had overlooked.

She wanted to indulge *herself.*

It was the first time Bronwen had experienced a physical reaction to the nearness of another. Sexual arousal, the books had called it. Until now it had remained a scientific term in her mind, one that explained why people sometimes behaved in ways that seemed quite mad.

Now she was personally acquainted with the power of the condition. It gnawed at her, making her restless and aware of her extremities. Her breasts ached. So did the juncture of her thighs and somewhere in the depths of her belly. Thinking of Tor and the way his gaze had lingered on her over supper made the sensations intensify.

She knew what she needed to do to address the ache, only a woman of good character did not take such pleasure for herself. If Reverend Jamieson of the Northallerton priory was to be believed, a good woman never felt such wicked impulses at all.

While the house grew quiet and still beyond her door, Bronwen wrestled with the immorality of what she was considering. To go to him would be wrong by every measure used to judge a lady.

Only Bronwen had put her back to societal expectations, so shouldn't such measures *also* be discarded? They were not empirical measurements. They were judgements. Reason said a normal woman would naturally experience such impulses.

Therefore, she was perfectly normal.

To appease such impulses, though…that was another matter altogether.

Only, she had been willing to do that this afternoon, when she had kissed him. For a moment, it had made perfect sense to her to follow the kiss through to the logical conclusion.

Tor had made her doubt. He had caused this confusion in her. He had made it seem like a good thing to refuse her. He had implied she was worthy of greater ambitions.

As Bronwen drew closer to his bedroom door, her heart stuttered and raced. She trembled. Was she being selfish?

She put her hand on the handle, took a breath and turned it. It was not locked.

The door opened without a squeak. There was normal lamplight within. The opening door revealed that Tor was still awake, despite the hour. He stood at the window, staring through the lace curtains, his arms crossed and his feet spread, scowling.

He looked around as the door opened and his eyes narrowed even more when he saw her. He had cast aside his jacket and waistcoat, collar and cuffs. He had put aside everything but his shirt and pants and boots.

Now he had seen her, her decision was cast. Bronwen made herself step inside and shut the door. Her trembling intensified as she pulled her wrapper about her tightly. "You have clouded the truth for me," she said, keeping her voice low. "I thought I knew what it was, that truth is a good thing. Isn't it a good thing? Is truth not the only measure worth using?"

Tor crossed the thick carpet to where she stood just inside the closed door. His blue eyes in the light of the single lamp looked black. "I hoped you would come. No, I wished it. I did not think even you would dare…"

He kissed her, stealing her breath. His hands caught her face once more. His fingertips stroked her cheeks and throat as his lips crushed hers. His tongue slid inside her mouth and played with hers.

All her careful reasoning evaporated. This was a truth more universal than any scientific principals or logic itself. Bronwen let go of any thought and enjoyed the sensations. His kiss was deep and thorough and made her whole body vibrate.

When he at last released her mouth, she gasped. "No, please don't stop!"

He shook his head. "I *should* stop. I should turn you around and push you out of the room and lock the door. If I were stronger, I would."

"I want you," she whispered. "You want me. Why must it be so complicated?"

"I don't know," he growled and kissed her again. "I only

know I can't stop thinking about you." His lips brushed her cheekbone before returning to her mouth and pressing against it once more.

The heat of his touch was electrifying. Bronwen didn't realize she had reached for him, until she felt the warmth of his shoulders under her hand, shielded only by fine cotton.

His lips trailed down her throat, to the opening of her wrapper. They slid over her skin, making her shudder violently in reaction. The tips of her breasts ached, only a few inches from where his mouth played.

Don't stop, please don't stop, she whispered in her mind.

"I wanted to throw aside the supper table tonight," he murmured, his arm sliding around her back, to hold her steady. "I wanted to rid myself of everything that lay between me and you. It was almost…savage."

Bronwen shivered again. "Stop talking," she said. "Talking confuses things."

"Yes," he agreed and swept her up off her feet and into his arms. He carried her over to the bed and placed her on it, then settled next to her.

Fear should be paralyzing her, yet it was absent. Instead, she wanted to hasten to the end, to experience it all. It wasn't intellectual curiosity. Her body's demands drove her onward. The power of the wanting was overwhelming. She wanted to tear her clothes away to hurry the matter. At the same time, she wanted to make the sensations linger.

Bronwen put her hand on his chest, against the soft pillow of flesh beneath the shirt and let her thumb stroke over the bare flesh showing between the open front. With a breath for courage, she pushed the shirt aside, revealing more.

The first fastened button prevented farther revelation.

Tor reached for the button.

"No, I'll do it."

He dropped his hand. "Other people have done such service for me, my whole life."

"I'm not doing it for you," Bronwen whispered, as she slid the button through the hole and released it. She drew a breath as the soft plane of his stomach appeared and eagerly unfastened the remaining buttons. She pulled the shirt aside, studying him.

"You find the view…appealing?"

"Very much."

His expression was impossible to read.

"You don't like that?" Bronwen asked, dropping her hands.

"I do, even though admiration of the human form is the province of men."

"And whores, I guess," Bronwen added.

"I wouldn't know about that," Tor said, his mouth turning up. He picked up her hand and placed it so her fingers spread across his torso. "I do know the look in your eyes when you study me is pleasing. I would have you do more of that."

"So would I," Bronwen confessed. "You are the first man I have found pleasing to look at."

His brow lifted. Then her secondary meaning registered.

He drew back. "You are…you really are innocent?"

"Innocent? No. I know what we do here, Tor. Don't look at me in that way."

"In what way?"

"You look horrified. This is my choice. You did not coax me here against my will…unless…is it that you find my lack of experience an impediment?"

Tor sat up. "I have never taken a woman's virtue. I don't know if I can." He lifted his head from his study of the bed cover. His gaze was direct. "It changes things."

"I don't see why," Bronwen said. She sat up, too. The heat and yearning in her was fading. Fear replaced it. Would he reject her now? Just because of a technicality?

"Of course it does," he shot back, his voice tight.

"Name one thing it changes that is not a silly society expectation," Bronwen demanded.

He remained silent, his jaw working.

"Well, then," she concluded.

"*You* would be different," he muttered. "So would I, for making that change in you."

"Would the change be negative?" she asked curiously. "I recall no such changes in my research."

"Research!" He said it as if it was a curse.

Bronwen considered him, startled. "Yes, you are right," she said, puzzling it out. "This is not the time or place for reason. I said talk spoils such moments, only a while ago. Very well. Let's not talk. It *does* trip us up. Instead, I will…"

She rose to her knees on the bed and tugged on the bow of the belt holding her wrapper closed.

I will follow my instincts and what my body tells me, instead of listening to my thoughts, she added silently. She removed the wrapper and let it drop behind her.

Tor held still. Even his breath halted.

Moving with a tense stiffness, he got to his knees, facing her. The open shirt fell aside, showing the band of his trousers, hanging loose about his hips with no braces to hold them. The skin looked soft and sensitive. Bronwen couldn't take her gaze away from the fine line of hair that arrowed into the trousers, darker than anywhere on his body. It was a siren song, begging for her to follow it.

Recalling a moment she had read in a salacious French novel, she reached up and slid the combs from her hair and shook it out. The tips brushed her rear. She shivered at the shadowy touch.

Tor let out his breath with a gusty sigh. "Dear *God*," he whispered.

Bronwen put her hand on her bare belly. "Stop talking," she reminded him. She wore nothing beneath the wrapper and now she trembled, not with fear, but with a growing excitement, as Tor's gaze moved over her. She could almost feel the heat in his eyes stroke her. The tips of her breasts didn't just ache, now. They hurt with the need to be touched.

She moved restlessly, her bare thighs shifting, making her even more aware of the heated flesh between them. Letting her instincts lead her, she picked up his hand and placed it against her breast and gasped at the contact of his hand against the tip.

With a groan he dropped his hand to her waist. He pulled her toward him, mashing her body against his and kissed her with a ferocious intensity, searing her mouth.

His hands against her bare flesh were heavenly. Bronwen let her head fall back with a sigh as his fingers slid down the back of her hip to the rounded flesh of her behind and cupped it. His lips released her mouth and moved over her chin and down her throat.

He trembled against her. The heat of him inside his trousers rubbed against her belly in a way that made her moan.

She fumbled with the fastenings that were in her way, her fingers mashed between them. She swayed back to give herself room.

Tor took the opportunity to dip his head lower. His mouth closed over the point of her breast and his tongue lapped at the pert tip.

Bronwen gave a choked cry and grabbed his head. She didn't know if she was trying to encourage him. She did know she didn't want him to stop. The delicious tugging and stroking sent ripples of pleasure through her, making the flesh between her thighs pulse and tingle. Her breath came in soft little pants.

She barely kept her eyes open, even though she wanted to see everything.

When he moved his mouth to her other breast, she groaned again. The need to finish this was a frantic ravening, making her shake with it.

Tor lowered her to the bed and lay over her, his lips not

leaving her breasts. His hands, now free, ran everywhere over the rest of her, wherever they could reach. He may have been exploring, only it was teasing to her. She wasn't sure she could withstand much more of it. There was a tension in her belly, deep in the core, that was building and growing. It was a piano wire winding tighter and tighter inside her, that quivered and shimmered with the tension, the merest touch of air making it whisper and vibrate.

When she reached for his trousers once more, Tor paused and lifted himself high enough to shrug off the shirt, as she opened the fastenings and let his trousers drop. With an impatient sound, he stripped his boots and the trousers from him and tossed them away.

Now he was naked, too.

Bronwen stared at the rampant shaft jutting from his thighs. His cock, she made herself call it, just in her mind. The curt Anglo-Saxon word was appropriate and made her heart skip a beat.

His cock was red with the blood that made it stand as it was. It was pulsing with the same beat as his heart.

As he rested over her, his cock brushing her thigh, she could see concern in his eyes. She rested her finger against his lips and shook her head. Then she drew him closer, her hands on his hips, guiding him. The sweet tension in her would allow nothing else. Even her thighs fell open, welcoming him.

Tor propped himself over her and lifted her knee, opening her up even more. The tip of his shaft pressed up against her aching, empty channel, then slid inside a little way. He paused.

Bronwen beat at his shoulder with her fist, little blows of frustration.

"Shh…" he whispered, even though she had not spoken. "This must be slow. I will not hurt you."

Bronwen didn't think he *could* hurt her. An unknown agency controlled her, driving her to finish this. She could barely lie still as he inched deeper into her. Her flesh separated around him, gripping him and squeezing in a way that made everything throb once more and made her groan, too. It was so very, very nice!

There was no pain, even though there was a tightness that resisted him for a few heartbeats. Then, as she breathed out a soft moan, the tightness eased and he drove himself deeper, then grew still.

The heat of his body against her was amazing.

Tor's gaze met hers. "You are…intoxicating," he whispered and touched his lips to hers.

Bronwen squeezed his shaft, her body rippling around him. Tor groaned. His hips thrust and he moved inside her. It was a glorious feeling.

"Do that again," she breathed.

He thrust again. Harder.

His arms flexed as he held himself up over her and drove into her over and over again. He would withdraw his cock slowly, then push deep again, with a soft grunt of effort that made her skin ripple. For long moments he continued, as her eyes drifted shut. The tension was building in her again, the piano wire tautness winding tighter.

Tor's movements grew faster, too. She opened her eyes, unwilling to miss a single moment of this glory.

Perspiration appeared at his temples, as he worked himself hard, pleasuring her. As the excitement built, she writhed beneath him, making soft little sounds that seemed to please him.

He clutched at the top rail of the bed, the tendons in his arm and neck flexing as he thrust, his body straining for the release she sensed was close.

Her release, too. It approached like a summer storm, crackling with energy and portent on the horizon.

Just a little more…

Then it arrived, stealing her breath and snapping her body as taut as the wire that had driven her here. Pleasure sparkled and flared, turning every nerve into molten sweetness.

Tor groaned and arched and held still, his hips moving in tiny little shifts, as his seed spilled inside her.

The release of tension was heavenly. Bronwen finally drew a full breath.

Tor sagged against her, his head dropping to touch hers. Then he stirred and withdrew from her body and lay next to her, his arm over her middle.

His heart was a fast staccato against her arm. As his breath slowed, he stirred. "Now I understand—"

She pressed her fingers to his lips once more. "No. Don't talk. No more talk. No more analysis. No more reason. There is no space for reason between us, not like this."

"I was about to say only that now I understand why I

had a headache, in peaceful Northallerton." He pressed his lips to her cheek. "I think I have wanted you for days now, buried deep where reason could not talk me out of it."

"While sensibility kept us blind to it," she added.

"Yes." His voice was low. "Bronwen——"

She kissed him, halting the flow of words. "Enough talk," she breathed into him. "I want to do that again."

He growled and kissed her.

Chapter Nine

When Doctor Thomas Rheems Mortenson came downstairs after his examination, he went straight to Rhys' study where Rhys waited with Anna.

Anna sat in her usual small chair by the desk, although she did not read. There was no book sitting next to her, either. The lace handkerchief in her hands had long ago torn. Bits of thread from the lace lay scattered over the front of her gown like rice at a wedding.

Rhys felt no corresponding joy, however. The formless, nameless cloud in his mind and heart made it hard to breathe. He couldn't abide the thought of sitting and waiting.

When Mortenson entered the room and Stamp shut the library door behind him, Rhys swallowed.

Mortenson put his tall hat and bag on the small table by the door. He was not smiling. Although it was often difficult to tell if he was smiling or not because his full dark beard and thick mustache hid most expressions. Only, his eyes were grave, now.

"Brandy, Doctor?" Rhys asked. His voice came out hoarse.

Mortenson shook his head. "I must be going. My wife is expecting me for dinner and I am already late..." He came forward. "I have finished my examination of Alice and the diagnosis is straightforward and simple."

"Please tell us, Doctor," Annalies said.

"Your daughter is very ill, I am afraid," Mortenson said. He hesitated.

Rhys' heart lurched and fell in a sickening way that made him gasp.

Mortenson licked his lips. "She has consumption," he finished.

Anna moaned. Rhys picked up her hand. His own was thick and unwieldy. He couldn't speak for the pain.

Anna drew in a breath that shuddered. Tears slid down her cheeks. "How long?" she whispered.

"Weeks only," Mortenson replied. "With proper care, perhaps a few months. Once you have adjusted to the news, we can discuss treatments. There is an asylum…well, no need to go into detail right now." He cleared his throat. "I will return on the morrow, Mr. Davies, if that is agreeable?"

Rhys nodded. He still couldn't speak. An invisible hand was gripping his throat and squeezing. He wouldn't know what to say, even if he could speak. How does one bid a formal goodnight to a man who had just delivered such devastating news? Polite expressions of fare-thee-well were torturous forms of hypocrisy.

Anna thrust herself to her feet even before Mortenson shut the door behind him and flowed into his arms. "Oh, Rhys!" she cried, her face against his shoulder. "My poor little Alice! She's only seventeen!" She sobbed silently, her tears soaking into Rhys' shoulder.

Wretched helplessness tore at him. Alice had always looked to him to fix toys, fix problems, find answers, solve things. Anna, too. Now here was something that threatened his daughter and he could do nothing at all.

Rage stirred, amidst the bewildered agony.

Pain, too. It tore down his arm, making him hiss and clutch at it.

Anna stumbled backward, her tear stained eyes wide. "Rhys?"

He *still* couldn't speak. The pain built. He grabbed at his chest as a lightning bolt ripped through it. Such agony! He had never experienced the like before.

Anna's hands were on his face, at his neck. He was sinking.

Falling.

"Doctor! Doctor! Stamp! Get Mortenson back here!" Anna screamed.

Her voice whispered to Rhys, close by his head. "Rhys, my love, please, look at me. The doctor is coming. Please, please, look at me."

Rhys tried to do as she asked, for he could hear the fear in her voice and he would remove that fear if he could. Protecting Anna, protecting his family, that was his work. His life. Only, he could say nothing. Do nothing. He had failed them.

In his mind, he screamed.

* * * * *

When Tor asked Jasper for a few moments of his time, Jasper instead invited Tor to travel with him on his daily visit to a tenant farm. Accordingly, Tor put on his borrowed boots and tramped across the fields in the early morning sunlight, his breath fogging the air in front of his face. Even in the two short weeks he had been staying at Northallerton, his wind had improved. He no longer found long walks taxing, although Jasper set a cracking pace across the fields, which offset the chill of the morning. It left no chance to talk.

Jasper visited a different tenant farm every morning. As there were thirty-three of them upon the Northallerton acres, it meant that Jasper would speak to every single farmer nearly every month. In winter, Jasper had explained, he reduced the visits to one every second day depending upon clement weather.

It was a simple, sensible management system that allowed Jasper to spot building trouble before it got out of hand. It generated goodwill—a fact that was not lost upon Tor. He watched Jasper greet the farmer, who was restacking hay bales in the barn, to make room for vulnerable cattle over the worst of the winter. The two chatted. The farmer was not servile, the way many of Tor's subjects were. He did not bow and scrape. He laughed and smiled and spoke about the weather, the winter culls and other aspects of a farmer's work.

The two of them spoke at length about crop rotation. Jasper was encouraging his tenant farmers to try crops of clover and peas to restore soils, instead of the ancient three-crop rotation system farmers had been following for generations. There was resistance to the new-fangled idea—Tor could see it in the farmer's reluctance, the way he rubbed at the back of his neck and plucked his sweaty shirt from his chest and shifted his muck-mired boots.

Jasper got his way, in the end. The winning argument was one of economics. More acreage could be planted each year with Jasper's new system, which meant bigger crops and more money. The farmer nodded and with a smile and a hand-shake, agreed to try the new system.

Although Tor suspected that the *real* winning argument was the farmer's trust in Jasper as his overlord. Jasper was liked and respected. The farmer had listened to him.

It was a thoughtful walk back to the house, for Tor could not help but draw comparisons. He could not name a single one of his subjects who had ever dared argue with him, when he had directed them to act in a way they did not find comfortable.

He wasn't sure he even knew *when* his people disagreed with him. Instant and total compliance with his wishes was automatic and expected.

Only, what if his wishes were wrong?

Uneasiness built in him. He unilaterally made decisions that affected the welfare of his people all the time. Yes, he drew upon the advice of experts and research, although once a new policy was decided, it was put into place and no one had ever pointed out if the policy was weak or needed changes or was even, perhaps, plain *wrong*.

Would a more democratic form of policy making, where feedback from the common folk helped shape future decisions…would that be more effective?

It was a novel concept, although it did not carry the shock it should have to a man raised in a family that had followed traditions for generations. Tor recognized Bronwen's influence. Without her mind-stretching ideas and attitudes, it never would have occurred to him to question the way rules and policies and laws were built in Silkeborg.

Thinking of Bronwen was a reminder of why he had sought Jasper's time this morning.

Bronwen... Just whispering her name in his mind tightened his sinews and made his heart hurry more than the swift walking was doing. The pit of his belly tightened with swift pleasure.

For five nights, now, she had come to him—sliding into the room like a white shadow shortly after the house had grown silent and still. Their nights together were feasts of erotic desire, for her curiosity knew no limits. Bronwen wanted to sample the pleasures of the flesh—*all* of them. Her self-directed education had not stopped at the borders of propriety.

She had deflected discussions about the ecstatic hours they laid together, despite Tor attempting to raise the subject many times. Bronwen would shut him down with a hand to his mouth, or something even more inventive—including, once, trailing her mouth down to his nether regions and applying her lips and tongue and teeth in a way that had stolen thought and breath and ability to speak.

They slept in small snatches throughout the night, in between bouts of lovemaking that left both of them trembling and weak. Then, in the morning, just before the rest of the house woke, she slipped out of his bed and returned to her room.

During the day, it was as if nothing had changed. Tor would have said the two of them had been left alone for long periods of time. It was an illusion. Now, when he wanted time alone with Bronwen, those moments were too short and too far apart. The butler and staff appeared without warning. Children frolicked with their aunt before racing off on a new adventure. Even Lilly appeared and sometimes Jasper, too, to exchange greetings and chat.

There had been one or two chances when Tor might have seized the moment to talk, except that Bronwen grasped the fleeting moment for herself. The first time they were alone in the library for longer than a few minutes, she pushed Tor back into the corner of the sofa and climbed onto his lap…and that was when he learned that beneath her lack of hoops and simple petticoat she wore nothing else. No pantalets or underdrawers prevented her from taking her pleasure. Tor was too astonished and too aroused by the sudden, stolen moment of eroticism to refuse her.

There had been other such moments. Once, inside a copse of trees, at the far north end of Northallerton. Once, up against the side of a stable, in full view of hundreds of black-faced sheep cropping peacefully nearby. Another memorable occasion had been in the storage closet beneath the stairs, amongst forgotten coats and walking sticks and one rusty broad sword that clattered when it fell. Those daytime moments were risky and unexpected and more powerful because of it.

The opportunity to insist upon discussing the nights with Bronwen did not appear.

Or perhaps, he acknowledged with wry candidness, he did not *want* the opportunity to occur.

He had only to look at Bronwen now, for his body to rouse and his shaft to rise to painful alertness. Thinking of her brought to him the memory of her subtle, spicy scent, which made his heart race and his body to throb.

How had he ever considered her to be a plain-looking woman? He understood why a man would think so. She was not a classical beauty. Her hair was a plain brown, her face neither thin nor round. Her eyes, though, were wells of knowledge and understanding, warmth and wickedness. Her skin was soft and lovely. He often could not stop himself from stroking it, over and over, marveling at the feel of it under his fingers. Her lips that did such inventive things to him, were not full and perfectly bowed. Instead, the corners would lift in a smile that appeared only for him. The sight of that tiny smile made his heart race, as he wondered what she was thinking…for unlike every other woman, Tor often had no idea what her fertile mind was considering from one moment to the next.

Contemplating the enigma that was Bronwen kept him occupied until they drew near the house itself. They approached the rear elevation, where the work yard and outhouses were grouped and the well-worn gravel path to the staff quarters cut through the field and trees.

There were many people milling about the yard, intent upon their duties. Stable hands were currying and tending horses, two maids were hanging linens to dry in the bright sunlight, for now the morning dew had evaporated, the sun was very pleasant. Kitchen hands were peeling vegetables and chatting, standing around an upturned barrel with their bowls and knives before them.

It was a hive of industry, a most domestic sight.

Jasper slowed as they stepped onto the path to the staff quarters and moved toward the house. "I should apologize. You wanted to talk, yet I have not provided an opportunity."

"It was an instructive morning, nevertheless," Tor said.

Jasper gripped his sleeve and drew him off the path once more. "Over here, in the sun. There's less chance of being disturbed here than in the house, where everyone knows where to find me."

The thick timbers that made up the exercise yard for horses made a suitably high support for leaning. The peaty smell of horses and manure was absent, for a small breeze was blowing, sending the scent of the sweet pea vines climbing the railing through the air.

Jasper looked at Tor expectantly.

Not for the first time, Tor saw the similarities in Jasper's face to his father's—the square jaw and strong neck. It was a reminder that he was speaking to a member of his family, despite the odd surroundings.

"I wanted to ask you about Bronwen," Tor began and halted. How to proceed with this matter without indiscretion?

Jasper's eyes narrowed. "What about her?"

"Her father," Tor began again. He shook his head. "This is a conversation I would normally leave to Baumgärtner, but needs must…" He made himself begin. "Her father is a commoner. I know that. Tell me he is the son of a king or petty prince. Tell me he has a high ranking connection in his parentage."

Jasper's gaze was steady. "Rhys is a bastard." His even tone reminded Tor that Jasper was also a bastard. "His father was a marquess. A minor one. The title is now moribund for there was no legitimate son and the attachments to the title don't allow it to pass through a daughter."

Tor took a deep breath, trying to ease his sinking heart. "I see."

Jasper raised a brow. "I'm afraid I do not. You were aware of Bronwen's parentage when you met her. Why do you seek further details now?"

Tor met Jasper's gaze. "I have…grown attached to her."

Jasper's gaze did not shift. "I thought so."

"You knew?" Horror touched him.

"You have not been indiscrete," Jasper assured him. "Only, you watch her. Whenever she is in the room." He gave a small shrug. "I remember doing that myself, once." His smile was small, but it was there.

"You still do, now and then," Tor told him, recalling the times he had seen Jasper watching his wife and the warmth in his eyes when he did.

"How strong is the attachment?" Jasper asked.

Tor held back his offense, warding it away with a reminder that he had begun this conversation. "Does it matter?" he asked with a neutral tone.

"If you were any other man, perhaps not," Jasper said. His tone was just as inoffensive as Tor's. "I have not speculated on the extent of your attachment, brother. Bronwen is…" Jasper smiled. "Bronwen knows her own mind. Beyond ensuring her health and safety, I do not intercede, as I know her parents wish it that way. I ask for no details now."

"Thank you."

"However, I am also my father's son. The illegitimate son," Jasper added. "There is a family history there that troubles me, now you have opened the subject and confessed the attachment."

Tor understood. "You think I seek a way to make her my mistress. On a more permanent basis."

"The possibility is there. It is not an uncommon practice, for those of rank."

"You misunderstand," Tor said. "I want a way to make her acceptable to the Council as my *wife*."

Jasper shifted on his feet, as if he had been surprised. He stared at Tor. Then he turned and plucked the last of the deep purple blooms from the vines, gathering them in one hand. "Do you love her, Tor?"

Tor blinked. "What on earth…?"

Jasper kept working. "It is a simple question. Do you love her?"

Tor cleared his throat. "Love is not a part of the equation," he said stiffly. "It is not a factor the Council can use to weigh her suitability."

"Oh. The Council." Jasper's tone was flat. He did not

meet Tor's eyes. Instead, he busied himself arranging the flowers in his hand.

"It is irrelevant," Tor added.

"Is it?" Jasper leaned against the fence once more, his hands and the blooms hanging over the top of it. He held them up. "Lilly likes sweet peas." Then he let them hang once more. "You seek a way to marry Bronwen because you consider yourself obligated?"

Jasper made it sound pathetic and weak. "I consider myself an honorable man," Tor countered.

"Then you *do* feel obliged," Jasper replied. He sighed. "Bronwen is the daughter of a bastard and a princess. Annalies' title also dies with her. Her father's principality no longer exists. She is cousin to the Queen, although the relationship is barely acknowledged. I estimate your Council will reel in horror if you were to put Bronwen's name before them."

Tor nodded, because Jasper's judgment was accurate. "It is as I suspected." His chest was tight, making it hard to breathe. "I do not know if there is a way forward, after this."

Jasper considered the flowers. "If you believe there is no way forward, then you will not see it when it presents itself."

Tor considered him, startled. "You don't understand. The laws of inheritance and security of the title are ancient practices that have ensured the title's existence for more than seven hundred years. To gainsay that wisdom…" He shook his head. "My will be damned," he added, his voice hoarse.

"As you say," Jasper replied. He turned as carriage

wheels and horse hooves clattered on the flagstones in the yard. A muddy brougham pulled up next to the dressed horses. "Why that's Appleton, from the telegraph office," Jasper said.

A young boy sitting next to the driver jumped to the ground and dug in the bag hanging on his hip. The boy waved a folded sheet of paper toward Jasper. "A wire, sir!"

As Jasper headed toward the boy, the driver descended slowly. He opened the door to the brougham and stood back and tugged the brim of his hat.

The man who stepped to the ground was silver-haired, his goatee pointed and his forehead high and smooth despite his age.

Tor stared at him, a sick blackness blooming in his chest.

It was Baumgärtner.

The Swiss man saw Tor and raised his brow, astonishment crossing his features. Then Baumgärtner remembered his place and bowed low. "Your Highness," he murmured, making the coach driver snap his head around to look at Tor and his mouth to drop open.

"Dear God…" Jasper breathed.

Tor turned. Jasper's face was pale, his gaze on the telegraph in his hand. "What is it?" he demanded. Everything was happening at once. The world circled him in tighter and tighter movements, snaring him and holding him in place, for daring to try to step off it.

"It's Bronwen's father," Jasper said, holding out the sheet.

Tor took it.

RHYS VERY ILL. BRONWEN TO COME AT ONCE. LETTER FOLLOWS. A.

Chapter Ten

When Rhys stirred, Annalies put the book she was not reading to one side and pocketed her spectacles. Her heart gave another of the funny creaks and squeezes it had been doing ever since Rhys' attack. She ignored it and bent over her husband's sickbed.

Rhys' skin had always been pale. Now it seemed transparent, tinged with a bruised gray about his eyes.

His eyes opened. "Anna...my love."

She picked up his heavy hand. "Rhys..." The tears threatened. Anna breathed through them. It would distress Rhys to see her cry. It always did. "You're awake again. Do you remember waking yesterday?"

He swallowed. "I'm alive."

"Yes, you're alive." She couldn't help but touch him. She pressed her hand to his face. "Rhys, my darling... Doctor Mortenson is most anxious to know something. Can I ask you a question?"

He licked his lips. "Yes."

"Did you have rheumatic fever when you were a child, Rhys? Do you remember being ill?" She held her breath, waiting for the answer. The heavy book she had put aside had told her why Mortenson was eager to know. Rheumatic fever weakened a person's heart, to the point where bad shocks like Rhys had suffered could kill them. It explained to Anna why Sharla's mother-in-law had dropped dead, last year, when presented with the facts of her son's marriage.

Rhys frowned. "No…" he breathed. "Never ill." His voice wavered.

Anna's relief was so great, she sank onto the bed next to him, her knees buckling. "You are quite sure?" she whispered.

"Yes. Mother proud of me. Robust, she said." Rhys lifted his hand, moving it as if it weighed heavily. He pressed his fingers to her cheek. "Don't."

She realized she was crying after all.

The bedroom door opened and Mortenson sailed in, his big bag in his hand. "What's this? What's this?" he demanded. "You shouldn't be here, your Highness. You'll put too much stress on his heart and upset him. Out you go! Out! Out!"

Anna rose to her feet. "I was just…"

Mortenson dropped his bag, his expression grave. "Do you not understand, your Highness, how emotional upsets can impede your husband's recovery?"

"I wasn't upsetting him!"

Mortenson squeezed her shoulder, his expression kinder. "You're distraught yourself, your Highness. A man of any empathy, and that includes your husband, will naturally feel a corresponding worry. For now, your duty must be to withhold from him all worry, all concerns, any hint of responsibilities and duties. Hysterical relatives, children, even concerned friends…their greatest kindness would be to leave him alone. Do you understand?"

Anna wiped her cheeks with her knuckles. "I've sent for

our sons and daughters…" Although, with Sadie in America, it might be weeks before she saw them once more. Even Bronwen was in Yorkshire, at least two days away.

"You must be firm with them, when they come," Mortenson said. "Rhys must not be excited in any way. Not for a good long while yet. Now…out you go, your Highness. I would tend my patient, if you please."

Anna moved out of the room, her mind turning, working hard, for the first time since Rhys had fallen.

* * * * *

Tor stayed by the window, out of the way of the family, as they tripped over each other and argued.

Baumgärtner sat in the big wing chair that was usually Jasper's seat, his cane between his knees and his hands resting on the silver knob. He did not move. Instead, his eyes followed the members of the family about the room. Often, they settled on Tor himself.

Tor knew the man was assessing his appearance and surmising a great deal from it. He did not care. Not now.

Bronwen was part of the little scene in front of the fireplace. She clung to the high mantelshelf, holding herself up, as she argued with Lilly and Jasper and the oldest child, Seth, clung to Lilly's skirt, his eyes big.

"The next train to London isn't until tomorrow," Bronwen pointed out. "I could rent a hack to get to York and catch the night train."

"A carriage to York would cost a small fortune!" Lilly

replied, aghast at such waste.

"I don't care!" Bronwen shot back. "I want to see my father!"

Jasper held up his hand, in a calming motion. "Not even if you left this instant, would you make York in time for the night train. That leaves tomorrow's train as the soonest, which you can catch if you leave here tomorrow at dawn."

The despair in Bronwen's eyes made Tor want to pull her into his arms and hold her, yet he could not.

He curled his fist and squeezed it, instead. He willed himself to look away from her.

The window he stood at looked upon the back yard. He watched as the same hack as this morning rolled into the yard and the same young boy jumped from the driver's bench and dug in his pouch.

"I believe there is another telegraph arriving," he said.

He didn't speak loudly, although he might as well have shouted, for the effect was the same. Everyone gasped and looked at him, with varying degrees of horror building in their faces.

Even Baumgärtner swiveled on his chair to glance around the high sides at him.

Jasper strode to the window and looked down just as the boy stepped into the service entrance of the house. "He's right," he said.

Lilly picked up Bronwen's hand and squeezed it.

Bronwen was a statue, motionless and white.

Jasper gave a soft curse, under his breath. "I can't wait for Warrick to get here," he muttered and strode to the door and opened it.

They listened as Jasper stepped across the slate in the front hall. Then nothing, for a long moment, while the room was still. No one spoke.

Jasper's boots grinding on the slate once more heralded his return. He stepped into the room, holding the wire. He held it out to Bronwen.

Her hand shook as she read it aloud.

"Rhys out of danger. Doctor says do not come. Stay in Yorkshire. Letter to follow. A."

"Oh, thank God!" Lilly breathed. "He'll live!"

Bronwen dropped onto the ottoman and put her face in her hands. Her shoulders shook.

Tor realized he had taken a step toward her when Baumgärtner looked at him sharply, his eyes narrowed. He made himself stay still, again. It took more discipline than he thought to stand and watch Bronwen's distress.

Jasper, though, was free to move. He lifted Bronwen to her feet and held her, patting her back and soothing her. "When the doctor says you can, I'll drive you to London myself to see him," he promised her.

"We both will," Lilly said, putting her arms around Bronwen too.

Even little Seth picked up her hem and held it.

Tor could not stand by a moment longer. He seethed with an aching need to *do* something.

He stalked from the room and from Baumgärtner's inspection…and away from Bronwen.

Chapter Eleven

The sun was setting on the long, exhausting day, when Bronwen next saw Tor. She had not noticed him leave the drawing room after the arrival of the second telegram. The little silver-haired man that Jasper had introduced to her as Baumgärtner had also disappeared when she next looked around her with any interest.

Warrick had served a late afternoon tea in the drawing room for no one showed any interest in moving into the dining room. They took their tea and scones on their laps and speculated about what might have happened to Rhys, for the promised letters would take days to reach Bronwen.

It was a useless, exhausting exercise, for nothing would be known for sure until the letters arrived. Bronwen curled up on the corner of the big sofa, her knees to her chest and her arms about her knees. She felt chilled. She clung to the hope imparted by the second telegram. Her father was out of danger.

When Baumgärtner returned to the drawing room, the polite little smile was missing. He nodded at Jasper. "Can word be sent to the hotel in town? The carriage should come at once."

"Now?" Jasper asked, startled.

"His Highness prefers to not linger while the family are dealing with personal upsets, as you are."

"I'll have Warrick see to it," Jasper murmured, moving

over to the bellpull and tugging on it.

Bronwen put her feet on the floor, as a tight band of pressure built in her chest. Tor was leaving. Tonight.

He could not leave! There was so much they had yet to say. To do.

Baumgärtner, though, settled on the front edge of the wing chair once more and put his hands on top of the cane, waiting. The posture, the readiness, told her that Tor really was leaving.

It took another hour for Tor to appear. He stepped into the room and shut the door behind him.

Bronwen sat up, her heart pattering hard, for Tor was a stranger to her.

He wore the suit she had first seen him in, now cleaned and pressed. The elegant lines of the black suit were a far cry from the rough woolen tweed he had been wearing only yesterday. His hair was brushed back neatly, his collar and cuffs white and stiff and finished with gold pins. His silk cravat, with the dull green fleck in it that matched his waistcoat, glowed in the mild red sunset light coming through the windows. His chin was shaved clean, removing the blond stubble he had delighted in rubbing against her flesh to make her writhe. His shoes gleamed.

Jasper got to his feet, putting aside the general medical text Bronwen had recommended to him. Lilly rose, too. Baumgärtner stayed where he was.

Tor looked at each of them in turn, except for Bronwen. Her heart picked up speed.

"With your permission, Jasper, I would have a last word

with Miss Bronwen," Tor said.

Jasper nodded. "Why don't you use the library?"

Finally, Tor looked at her. "Bronwen?"

She nodded.

Tor turned and left.

Bronwen hurried after him, her stomach cramping and her heart slamming against her chest. She thought she would have to chase him all the way to the library, yet he stood just beyond the door to the drawing room, waiting for her.

Then she understood. The distance, the coolness, had been for Baumgärtner's sake.

She reached for his hand.

Tor pulled it out of her reach and shook his head.

Fear bloomed, large and dark. Bronwen swallowed.

"The library at least has a door we can close," Tor said. He moved across the hall, then turned and waited for her to walk by his side.

Bronwen followed him through the wide corridor to the big library door and stepped inside. Warrick always kept the fire burning until the late evening, in case she chose to use the library at night. It was crackling and popping now, for someone had just laid fresh logs on the embers.

It was the only sound in the room, except for the closing of the door.

Bronwen couldn't make herself move beyond the door. Her legs would not cooperate.

Tor, though, moved over to the leather tucked armchair and perched on the arm, as he had done on his first day at Northallerton.

The return of that stiff, upright man explained to Bronwen more thoroughly than any book could that Tor—the Tor she knew—had in all ways but physical left her already.

Only, her heart would not let her accept that.

"Bronwen…"

"Is there nothing for us?" she asked. "No hope at all?"

"I must return to my duties. Silkeborg needs me."

"*I* need you."

Tor swallowed. Where his hands gripped his arms, his knuckles showed white. Only, his expression was distant. Regal. "There is no hope for us," he said, his voice soft. "There never was. You must have known. You *did* know. You know everything."

I know I love you. The words hovered on her lips. Pride made her force them back.

There was one last chance for her. She had wrestled with it for the last hour, while waiting for Tor to return to the drawing room. "Jasper's mother and your father—"

"No." He snapped the word.

Bronwen recoiled, astonished at the anger in his voice.

Tor got to his feet. "I know what is in your mind. I will not have that life—that ignoble, ignored life—I would not wish that upon you, not even if it gives me what I want."

Her eyes pricked, heralding tears. She hated crying and she would die if her tears fell where Tor could see them. Bronwen blinked hard. "Then you do not care enough to keep me even as your mistress?"

Tor swore, making her step back another inch or two. He could only have learned that word from the local farmers. She had never heard him curse before.

He came toward her, moving slowly, as if he fought for every step. "What I feel, however I might care, has nothing to do with this," he said, his voice low. "It cannot influence my decision. Do you understand? There are greater forces at work here, that drive me back to Denmark. Tell me you understand that."

"Of course I do." Bronwen hesitated. "Do you care, then? Even a little?"

His chest rose and fell. "Don't ask me that."

"Then you will give me nothing to keep from this," she said bitterly.

"God help me," Tor breathed. "You don't understand. You, who knows everything and sees all...*now* you do not understand."

Bronwen shook her head. "No, I don't!" she cried. "Tell me the *truth*, Tor! Tell me this was something more than a... a distraction!"

"No!" He clenched his fists, breathing hard. "To say anything at all...don't you see? It would not be a kindness."

Bronwen let out a shuddering breath. "Your father *loved* Jasper's mother. He told her so, over and over again, until she died."

"And that is all of him she had," Tor shot back. "Empty words." He shook his head. "Look at us, Bronwen. *Really* look, I mean. See the distance that is already between us."

She didn't have to look to know what he meant. She had sensed the difference as soon as he had walked back into the drawing room in his fine suit and elegant appointments.

Bronwen wore one of her oldest muslin dresses, with stains about the hem from walking across muddy fields. The cloth was thin from too many washings and the green sprigs faded.

It wasn't just clothes that separated them, though. They were from two different worlds.

"If I speak, if I say anything, then I would condemn you to the same empty life that Jasper's mother lived," Tor said. "I would not wish that upon you, Bronwen. I will not be the one to cut short your wonderful freedom and restrict you to a hollow, loveless existence, waiting in hope for a return that will never happen. So I will end this now. Here. You must live your life as fully as you planned."

"What if I don't want that life anymore?" she whispered. Her heart was breaking. She could dispute nothing he said.

"Find another man who will give you his love," Tor ground out. "Mine will only destroy you."

He walked to the door, moving stiffly.

Bronwen could not leave it there. She caught at his fist. "Tor…"

He caught her head in his hands and kissed her.

Bronwen clung to him, soaking up every last sensation of the deep, wonderful kiss, for she knew it was the last.

Then, Tor plucked her hands from his jacket and put them by her sides. For a moment, his blue eyes looked into hers.

Then he turned and left, closing the door behind him.

Bronwen stood where she was for a long time after he left, her lips still tingling with the touch of his. She didn't think. She stood, wishing the ground would swallow her whole.

When carriage wheels and horse shoes crunched on the gravel outside, Bronwen stirred.

She ascended the iron stairs to the second floor, where the high windows were. She pushed the rolling ladder over to the closest window and climbed it. The library cases that stood beneath the window provided a two-foot wide ledge she climbed onto and kneeled to peer at the front of the house.

There were *three* carriages standing there. Two of them were broughams, with a pair each. The carriage between them was a grand coach with a coat of arms on the black varnished door and four horses to pull it.

Warrick's footmen stood at attention in front of the house, while liveried footmen climbed from the carriages. They even wore wigs.

One of the liveried footmen helped a woman climb from the big coach. The woman was slender and blonde and wrapped in a blue velvet traveling cloak with white fur trimming. At the front opening of the cloak, silver silk peeped. She wore the same elongated hoops that Sharla was wearing and insisting were the latest in French fashion. The hem of the dress was embroidered with dark gray flourishes and curlicues. There was not a spot of mud or dirt anywhere on her.

The woman stepped on to the gravel and put the hood back up over her glowing blonde hair. She pushed her hands into a fur muff and turned her head to examine Northallerton with a critical eye.

There was a sound of voices from the big front door and light spilled onto the gravel. Warrick came out, carrying the big lamp.

Then Jasper and Tor emerged onto the gravel in front of the coach.

The woman pulled her hands from the muff and hurried forward, lifting them toward Tor. Bronwen heard her speak, although the words made no sense. *Danish*, she reminded herself.

The woman hurried to Tor and reached up and kissed his cheeks, both of them, still talking, her voice soft as honey.

Bronwen gripped the iron clasp of the window until it bit into her palm.

Tor had spoken of the parade of suitable women being presented to him. This was another, except her familiarity with him said she was related. Another cousin, for Tor had no sisters or brothers, except for Jasper.

The footmen snapped to attention at Tor's appearance. The one who had helped the lady to the ground stood back with the coach door held open.

Tor stopped at the door and turned to speak to Jasper. Quiet words that Bronwen could not hear.

Jasper nodded. Then he stepped back and bowed.

Of course. Tor was the Archeduke Edvard Christoffer.

Tor shook his head with an impatient movement. He closed the distance between them and hugged Jasper, in front of everyone.

Bronwen pressed her fingers to the cold glass, her heart hurting.

Jasper clapped Tor on the shoulder, then Tor climbed into the coach.

The woman was helped up into it behind him, then Baumgärtner stepped up with difficulty, his cane working.

The door was dogged shut and with a cry of command, the three carriages rolled into motion. They turned in a big circle and headed for the road to the village.

Did he watch the house to glimpse her? Bronwen didn't know, for she couldn't see. Her tears blinded her.

＊ ＊ ＊ ＊ ＊

Lilly waited by the fire until Jasper returned from outside. She held her hand out to him. "Poor Bronwen!" she breathed, as he took it. His hand was cold, telling her the chill of winter was here. She pulled Jasper closer to the fire.

"Tor was right," Jasper said, holding his hands out to the flames. "There is no possible future for them. It's better to make the cut now. Although…there may yet be long term consequences we must deal with."

Lilly stared at him. "A child?" she breathed. "Surely, Bronwen would not be so foolish—"

Jasper laughed and pulled her into his arms and kissed her forehead. "My love, *you* were that foolish, remember?"

Lilly rested her head on his shoulder. "That was different."

"Was it?" His voice rumbled against her cheek in a very

agreeable way. "Neither of them are in a position to reveal their true feelings."

"Oh dear." Lilly lifted her head. "We must be kind to Bronwen, now."

"Yes, we must." He pulled her back against him. "Although this whole affair and Rhys' misery, too...it has reminded me of how very lucky I am to have you."

She rested her hand on his chest. "And I, you, my love."

Jasper lifted her chin. "We should not forget the lesson," he said, his voice low. "I think we should try again."

"For another baby?" The faded memory of tiny George lying still in his crib, the last sight she'd had of him, flickered through her mind and stirred her heart.

"Yes, another baby," Jasper said. "Life goes on. Let's not waste it. Let's give another baby a chance for a full life that only we can give them."

Lilly's heart filled. "Yes," she breathed. "To share all we are so very lucky to have. Yes, we must."

"I love you, Lady Lillian," he murmured and kissed her.

Chapter Twelve

Rhys had grown to hate the sight of snow falling upon London's streets. It was a sign of mushy, muddy days ahead and a coldness in the air that chilled the bones. Now, though, as he sat watching snow fall through the window of the upstairs sitting room, he decided he had never seen anything so wonderful in his life.

It was wonderful *because* he was watching it fall.

"It's snowing," he whispered.

Anna put down her book and took off her spectacles and looked through the window. "How lovely! I do like the first snowfall of the year." She reached and picked up his hand where it rested on the arm of the chair and squeezed it.

Rhys was able to squeeze back, a massive milestone in his recovery. For weeks, he had been unable to hold anything and had to be helped to sit up in the bed. Now he could shuffle a few steps by himself into the sitting room, to fall exhausted into the chair by the fire.

Benjamin reported to him every day, there by the fire. He would summarize the business affairs of Davies, Baker & Sutcliffe, Rhys' law firm on Middle Temple Lane, before returning to the Wakefield townhouse in Grosvenor Square for the evening. It had taken Rhys many months to understand the domestic arrangements in the Wakefield house, for Ben had been closed-mouthed about it. When Rhys had arrived at the truth, he had been astonished and mildly offended.

Anna snapped him out of his squeamish distaste. "If I had been married off to a prince in Europe, you would be in the same position as Benjamin, Rhys. Do not turn your nose up at his happiness. All *three* of them are blissfully happy with the arrangement. You cannot judge. They are not flouting it about London and they are preserving their reputations."

"Except all of London will eventually know," Rhys pointed out, perplexed at his wife's far more forgiving nature in this matter.

"All of London may suspect, only no one will know for certain, except the family and none of us will say anything to outsiders. You know how it goes."

Benjamin's supreme contentedness had confirmed to Rhys that the unconventional arrangement did seem to work for them. From observing Sharla and her husband, the Duke, Rhys was finally able to put the matter to rest in his own mind. No one was suffering. No one was unhappy. If that was so then, indeed, who was he to judge?

He instead enjoyed being able to squeeze his wife's fingers, even a little and be glad for the snow falling.

"It will soon be time for afternoon tea," Anna observed, glancing at the clock on the mantel shelf. "Would you like to stay up after tea? Maybe see if you have the strength to last to dinner, tonight?"

"I do feel stronger, today," Rhys admitted. He sighed and glanced through the window. "I am *trying*, at least."

"There is no rush," Anna replied. "You can take as

much time as you need."

Rhys laughed. It came out wheezy. "I can't take forever," he pointed out. "The offices will not run unattended for long."

Anna froze.

"What did I say?" Rhys asked, alarmed.

Anna got to her feet, her blonde locks, that she had let down in the privacy of their own sitting room, swung with her movement. With stiff motions she stepped to the door, then back again.

"Anna?"

She dropped in front of his knees and rested her hands on the blanket covering them. "Rhys, my darling…you cannot go back to work. Not ever."

Rhys stared at her. His heart stirred, which added to his fright. Mortenson insisted upon avoiding shocks and efforts, of pacing himself. "Not work?" he repeated, his lips numb.

"Benjamin is more than capable of running the business now," Anna said. "I've listened to his daily reports. They're boring, because he is managing things perfectly well. The office *can* run without you now, Rhys."

"What would I do?" he asked, flummoxed.

"Whatever you want," Anna said swiftly. "How often have you spoken of traveling? Europe? Even America. Sadie is there." Her eyes glittered. "Let me take you and Alice away from here. Somewhere warm, where we can be together for…a while."

Rhys closed his eyes, wretchedness pulling at him. "Alice…"

Anna shook his hands. "You must retire, Rhys. Leave your affairs to Ben and the others. It's their turn now."

Rhys shook his head. "Old men retire," he whispered.

Anna got to her feet. "I love you, Rhys Davies. I will not sit idly by and watch you work yourself into an early grave. I insist you retire, so I can love you when you *are* an old man!"

Her tears welled and fell, yet she did not make a sound.

Rhys held his hand out to her. "Shh…shh…my love, yes, if that is what it takes to make you happy, then I will retire."

Anna did sob, then. She rested her head on his knee and wept while he soothed her. To be able to stroke the faded gold locks of her hair made him profoundly grateful. He would do whatever she asked to keep doing so for many years to come.

That was how Stamp found them, when he delivered the letter from Lilly, about Bronwen.

* * * * *

After the flurry of the Princess' arrival, greetings, inspection of children and hugs and kisses, Warrick poured Lilly and Annalies tea and left them in the morning room.

The Princess got up from her elegant pose on the chair and stood in front of the fire. She pushed her hoops aside and put her foot on the guardrail, like a man, with her elbow on the mantelshelf.

Lilly smiled at the display. It was just what Bronwen

would do, if she were here.

"Where is Bronwen?" Annalies asked, rubbing her brow.

"She is either out walking, or in her room," Lilly said. "Since the Archeduke left, she has not once stepped inside the library, when she would spend all her days there."

Annalies winced. "To cut herself off from books…this is bad, Lilly. Tell me about their association. Tell me everything."

Lilly sighed. "I would be guessing at most," she confessed. "They were both more discreet than the grave."

"Then speculate," Annalies said. "I cannot help her if I do not know what ails her. Tell me about…Tor, did you say he calls himself?"

"What he asked we call him," Lilly replied. "Apparently, only his father ever used the name."

Annalies' direct gaze met Lilly's. "That is interesting, isn't it?"

Lilly sighed. "He is an interesting man…" she began.

* * * * *

"Bronwen. Wake up. Bronwen, sweetheart. Time to wake and speak to me."

The voice was familiar. Bronwen roused reluctantly, for sleep was such a pleasant retreat. She preferred the long moments before sleep took her, when the weight of the world slipped away and she floated, unfeeling, drowsy and warm.

She could hear Tor's voice in such moments. She could remember his hands upon her with a clarity that was denied her upon waking.

"Bronwen!" Sharper this time.

A hand on her arm. Shaking her.

There was no defense against the physical assault that would let her stay asleep. Bronwen opened her eyes with grudging slowness.

Her mother stood over her. It was her mother who shook her so forcefully.

Bronwen blinked at her. "Mother? What are you doing in Yorkshire?"

"I came to see you," Anna said briskly. "Lilly wrote and said you were in need of assistance."

"I don't need help, thank you," Bronwen whispered and closed her eyes.

Bitingly cold water splashed against her ear and cascaded down her arm, running beneath the warm cocoon of blankets.

Bronwen gasped and sat up, staring down at the puddle of water soaking through the fabric of her nightgown and wetting her thighs.

Annalies stood over her, the water pitcher held up high over her head.

"Mother!" Bronwen cried. "What on earth…!"

"That's better," Annalies said, putting the pitcher back on the washstand next to the bowl. She brushed her hands. "Dress yourself and meet me in the library. We have things to discuss."

"No, not the library," Bronwen said, her heart twisting.

Her mother paused at the door. "Very well, then. I am

sure Lilly will spare us her morning room for a while. If you do not present yourself there in ten minutes, then I will beg the cook for a bucket of her slops and dowse you in that, instead."

Annalies shut the door behind her and Bronwen shuddered. She did not doubt for a moment that her mother would do what she threatened if Bronwen did not appear downstairs within the stated time limit.

She threw the sodden blankets aside and stripped off the soaked nightgown. Her underthings would not slide over her damp skin. She cast them aside with an impatient hiss, aware of time ticking away. Her dress, the faded muslin, was too thin to wear over nothing. Instead, she pulled the traveling suit from the wardrobe and struggled into it. It was a wrapper style dress, which she could fasten at the front, only the worsted wool was prickly against her skin. There was no time to select another. She tugged her hair out of the collar, pulled up the fronts out of the way and pinned them without consulting mirror and tugged her sleeves into place. She didn't bother with shoes, despite the deep cold gripping Yorkshire. There was no time.

Her heart racing, Bronwen hurried down the stairs and into the morning room.

Lilly sat behind her desk. She put the pen down and capped the inkpot.

Annalies stood with her hand upon the chair in front of the desk, her other fist against her waist. If she had not been wearing hoops, Bronwen suspected her mother would have her fist planted on her hip, instead.

"I will give you the room," Lilly murmured, stepping out around the desk.

"You are family, Lilly," Annalies said. "You do not have to leave if you do not wish to."

Lilly cleared her throat, then looked at Bronwen. "Would you like me to stay?"

Bronwen struggled to care one way or another. She gave a small shrug. "If you wish."

Troubled, Lilly returned to her desk. "Perhaps a neutral witness may help," she said, pushing a curl back into place behind her head with an awkward movement.

Annalies patted the chair. "Sit if you wish. I understand you have not been active lately. Perhaps standing will strain you."

Bronwen could feel her cheeks heating. She stayed just inside the door.

Annalies let her hand drop from the back of the chair. "First things first. Are you with child?"

The bald question, asked aloud, with Lilly watching, should have filled Bronwen with mortification. Her *mother*, asking such a question?

However, no humiliation arrived. Instead, a soft little cry sounded in her mind. Her eyes ached. Blurred. "I hoped I was," she whispered. "Yet I cannot have even that much of him."

Silence sounded. Bronwen did not care if she had shocked them. She had spoken the truth. It was not her fault if they chose to be offended by it.

She felt her mother's hands on her arms. "Come along,

my dear," Annalies said softly. "Come and sit. I had not realized how deeply this ran. Come." She guided Bronwen to
the chaise longe and settled next to her.

Bronwen wiped her cheeks, trying to clear her vision
once more.

Her mother picked up her hand. "You are in love with
him, yes?"

Bronwen looked down at the scratch wool over her
knees. "Is that what I am? It hurts to be awake and now he
isn't here and will never be."

"He told you that?" Annalies asked.

Bronwen nodded.

Annalies tucked her hair behind her ear, her movements
gentle. "Would you tell me everything that happened, darling? I can help, if I know…well, not *all* the details, but the
important ones, at least."

Because she didn't care anymore, Bronwen told her.
Everything. As she spoke, her energy returned. It was a relief to speak of it aloud.

Lilly moved about the room as she spoke and whispered
to Warrick at the door. A plate of roast beef sandwiches appeared. Bronwen gulped them down, her hunger stirred by
the sight of them.

It took time to tell her mother everything. The carriage
clock on the desk chimed twice while she was speaking.

Lilly handed her another plate, this one with fruitcake
and preserves. Bronwen ate that, too. She couldn't remember the last time she had eaten something. The rum-ladened
fruit cake was ambrosial.

While she ate, her mother circled the floor in tight arcs.

Lilly returned to the desk. "Tor was far more considerate than I understood. Thank you for explaining to us, Bronwen." Her gaze shifted to Annalies. "Your Highness?"

"'Highness'?" Annalies repeated and rolled her eyes. "Ha!"

Bronwen put the plate aside. "Mother, are you angry with me?"

"I am angry with my stiff-necked, snobbery-oriented relations!" Annalies cried, throwing out her hand. "The devil hang their privileged hides!"

Lilly's mouth opened.

Bronwen felt her mouth twitch toward a smile.

Her mother whirled, her hoops swaying. "Of course you are good enough for the man! You are my daughter, a descendant of the royal house of Saxe-Coburg-Weiden." She raised her hands to her head, as if it ached. "That blonde cousin you saw, the one who greeted Tor so intimately? I know who she is and let me tell you, she is less royal than you, darling daughter. I'm given to understand that she is… well, from the wrong side of the blanket."

"Really?" Lilly asked, her interest pricked.

Annalies smiled. Her smile was full of devilment that astonished Bronwen. She could easily imagine her mother slipping through London in men's clothes, as it was rumored she once did.

"Let me say she looks nothing like her father and very much like her father's former secretary, a man who was dishonorably discharged from the French army."

Bronwen wrung her hands. "Nevertheless, Tor is right. We are both from two very different worlds. Even if you could somehow make his council agree to the match…" She halted. "How silly to think they would ever agree to such a thing!"

"That *is* the silly part of it," her mother replied. She flopped onto the chaise next to her. "Tor was a most considerate man. He said it himself. He would not make you give up the freedom you have spent years fighting to preserve." Anna picked up her hand once more. "That is a choice *you* must make, my dear."

"I?" Bronwen swallowed. "You mean, I could just… *choose* to belong to his world? Just like that?"

Annalies nodded. "The truth is, you are already a part of his world, by virtue of your birth. You are as much a part of his world as the woman in blue velvet. You only have to step into it."

"How do I even begin to do that?" Bronwen asked, her heart beating with a wild hope. "I mean…that woman…and then…me…" She plucked at the itchy wool.

"You have a decision to make before we deal with the details," Annalies said, her tone brisk once more. "Is this something you want, Bronwen? *Truly* want? Do you understand how your life must change, if you chose this path?"

Bronwen pressed her lips together, thinking of the woman in blue velvet. "I must rejoin society," she said.

"Not just rejoin it," Lilly said. "You must win it over, so that no one will even think to object to your antecedents."

"As you did, Lilly?" Bronwen asked.

Lilly smiled. "I had Jasper to help me." Her face glowed.

"While you, my dear, must…" Annalies frowned. "What is that military expression that Jasper uses, Lilly?"

"Ambush?" Lilly supplied.

"That is not the word I was thinking of, although it will do nicely," Annalies replied.

"I must ambush Tor?"

"He will resist you, because he believes you want this—" She waved her hand to include the room, the house and the land beyond it. "A life in the wilds, left alone to read and think. He won't take that from you. You must convince him you want *his* life more."

"How can I do that?" Bronwen said. "I don't know if I want it at all!"

"Do you want Tor?" Lilly asked.

"Yes!"

Her mother nodded. "That is enough for now. Put yourself on the path and the rest will resolve itself later."

Bronwen breathed in and let it out. She felt light and airy, as if she could float. "Can you help me, Mother? Can you show me the way?"

"Me?" Her mother sat back. "I am the absolute *worst* person to show you *that* path, my dear! I would rather read books and traipse about just as you do."

Bronwen's heart fell.

Annalies patted her hand. "However, I do happen to know two ladies who are just the right people to help."

Chapter Thirteen

Silkeborg, Denmark. December, 1865.

Walking in a snow-heavy forest was not the same thing as walking the hills and dales of Yorkshire, especially when one was wearing hoops and petticoats and all the layers of undergarments necessary to be considered well-dressed. Bronwen tried to contain her petty frustration as the lace on her petticoat snagged once more on the rough bark of a fir tree. She looked around to see if anyone was within sight, then bent from the waist to unsnag the hem, instead of crouching, as a lady would.

Her bend was arrested before it began, as her corset dug into her hips and under her arms at the unnatural movement required of it.

With a sigh, she straightened up once more, then bent her knees and sank to the level necessary to work the lace free.

She paused when she saw a delicate plant hugging the southern base of the tree, tucked into a warm pocket of earth made in the snow by the fall of the sun through the canopy. The leaves were familiar to her.

"Angelica," she whispered, remember Agatha's lessons about wild angelica. The forest around Silkeborg was a herbalist's delight, with many herbs and medicinals growing wild that were not native to Britain. She could collect and dry herbs for a year and still not have enough.

Only, she was not in Denmark to harvest plants. With a sigh, she left the angelica alone and rose to her feet, her petticoat free. She had been walking for the single hour her mother had allowed. It was time to return to the town.

She set off as briskly as possible, tracing her footsteps back through the snow. Here in Denmark, the snow remained thick and white throughout winter, making the landscape a pale blanket of interesting lumps and bumps. Under the trees, the snow thinned, although it did not disappear altogether.

It was a very different landscape to Yorkshire and utterly different compared to urban London. Even the silence that came with the thick covering of snow was unique. She heard the crunch of snow under her boots and the soft note of wind in the tops of the trees, far overhead.

It took little time to reach the edges of the town. Silkeborg was a small place, no larger than Northallerton, yet it was the seat of a duchy. Bronwen walked along the river tow path, watching the blue-green water tumble over the shallows, before turning into the main street and walking to the Magistrate's house.

The butler nodded formally. He knew no English and Bronwen's Danish was limited.

"The Princess?" she asked him.

He pointed to the room that Bronwen had decided was a drawing room, although it had nothing but upright chairs with flat seats and slatted backs and a plain wooden table.

It was not the dining room, for *that* room was considerably warmer and more comfortable. They ate their meals there. Hr. Fisker, the Magistrate and their host, greeted his guests and associates in the dining room, too. He sat by the huge white stove, his feet propped on the rail in front of it, warming his toes, while guests pulled up chairs next to his big armchair.

This plain drawing room went unused, except for their party of English women, who must puzzle the household with their constant requests for tea.

Bronwen pushed the door to the drawing room open as she removed her gloves and bonnet. Then she remembered to turn and give the butler her things. She smiled at him.

He gave her another bow and carried them away.

With a sigh over the endless details she must remember to pay attention to now, she went inside.

Her mother was reading a letter, her spectacles sitting on the edge of her nose.

Lady Natasha and Lady Elisa were both at the table, playing cards. They looked up when Bronwen entered.

"Right on time," Elisa said approvingly, glancing at the clock.

"You have stray hair about your ears, too," Natasha said.

"Oh." Bronwen brushed the curls out of the way.

"No, work them into the side hair with your fingertips, as I showed you," Natasha told her. "Or you will spend the rest of the day fighting them."

"Yes, of course. Thank you," Bronwen said, weaving the strays back in and smoothing them over with her fingers. She brushed down her dress, arranging the folds over the hoops. They were the French kind, wider at the back than the front, just as Sharla had said were the fashion in Paris, for they had been bought in Paris. Every garment she wore had been acquired in Paris, in a whirlwind two days of shopping with Natasha and Elisa that had left Bronwen exhausted and nervous in a way that even the most strenuous walking had never done.

"Is there word from the palace?" Bronwen asked her mother.

Annalies held up her hand for silence. "Let me finish," she murmured.

From somewhere deeper inside the house, an abject groan sounded. It seeped through the walls.

"What *is* that noise?" she asked, startled.

"Hr. Fisker," Natasha said, frowning at her cards.

"The Magistrate?" Bronwen said. "He is not in court today?"

"Apparently not," Elisa replied.

The groan sounded again. The note of pain in it made Bronwen shift uneasily.

Annalies folded the letter with a flick of her wrist. "The Archeduke and his retinue are in Belgium."

"Belgium?" Elisa repeated. "Why?"

"Are they insisting he finish that silly tour of his?" Bronwen asked.

Annalies shook her head. "While we were in Paris, King Leopold died. They have gone to Belgium in anticipation of the coronation of the new king."

"Was Leopold a cousin of yours, Mother?" Bronwen asked.

"Not directly, although I'm sure if you count back far enough we have ancestors in common," her mother replied.

As the groaning sounded again, Bronwen frowned. "And you had to learn that from Father, in Britain? We might have discovered it ourselves, if we had gone to the palace, instead of sitting here for two days."

"Oh, you cannot simply call upon the palace," Elisa said, for protocol and etiquette were her specialties. "You must be *presented* and not by just anyone."

"Very well, then," Bronwen said, irritation flaring, for the groaning was growing louder. "We should go to Belgium, then."

"Not without an invitation," her mother said firmly.

"You are the last heir of the Principality of Saxe-Weiden," Bronwen pointed out. "They would not invite *you?*"

"They have not, so far," Annalies said, her tone still eerily calm. "You must have patience, Bronwen. All of Europe comes to a halt when a head of state dies. In the new year—"

"We must stay here for *Christmas?*" Bronwen asked, appalled.

"It very much depends on when the new king is crowned. It is winter, my dear. Travel can be difficult to manage."

"Moldering bodies are even more difficult to manage," Bronwen pointed out, her teeth together.

Elisa looked shocked. Natasha, though, smothered her laughter behind her cards, her eyes dancing. "She is *just* like you, Anna!"

The pitiful groan sounded once more, drawn out into a wail that made her skin crawl. Bronwen could stand it no longer. She whirled and marched out into the front room of the small house, then over to the door to the dining room. She pushed it open and stepped in.

Hr. Fisker was bent over in his chairs, his hands to his stomach. When he saw Bronwen, he straightened and glared at her. "You have need of something, my Lady?" His English was bad enough that they had stopped trying to explain that even though she was the daughter of a princess, she was not a lady, but merely Miss Davies. The intricacies of the English peerage appeared to be only slight less complicated than the Danish branch.

Despite trying to stand, Fisker could not manage it.

Bronwen sank in front of him and looked at his face. "You are in pain," she said. She pointed to where he clutched his belly. "It hurts." She reached for her own stomach and grimaced as if she was in pain.

"No, no," he said. "It is nothing."

"I can help," Bronwen assured him. "Let me see."

"Undskyld mig?"

Bronwen had learned the phrase meant, roughly, 'excuse me?' for many of the locals used it when she attempted to speak to them.

Instead of repeating herself, she reached for his hand and pulled it away from his stomach, to give her access. A simple probing with her fingers would tell her if the stomach was bloated, or if something more sinister was at work.

He winced, hissing.

She looked at his hands, at the misshapen ends of the fingers. "Oh…" she breathed, studying them. "*This* is what ails you. This is why you sit by the fire. The heat helps." She tapped the toe of his boot. "Your toes, too, yes?"

He looked at her miserably, pain in his eyes. She suspected he would groan again, if she were not here.

Bronwen put his clawed hand back on his lap and patted the back of it. "I can help." She stood up, sifting through her memory for every tidbit Agatha had ever given her on the treatment of rheumatism, plus anything she recalled from her own reading.

"Angelica," she murmured. She bent in front of the Magistrate once more. He stared back, beads of perspiration on his temples. "Does your cook have dry angelica in the kitchen?"

"Angelica?" he repeated, puzzled. He shrugged.

"Black current seed oil?"

He stared back.

"Borage?"

He wrinkled his nose. "*Ukrudtsplante*," he muttered. He frowned. "Weed," he added.

"Not to you, it isn't," Bronwen assured him. She held up her hand. "I will be right back."

She hurried through to the drawing room. The three women looked up as she stepped inside.

"Aunt Elisa, you must write to Sharla for me," Bronwen

told her.

"Goodness! Why must I do that?" Elisa asked, as she reached for her folder of stationary.

"I need every ounce of that turmeric her mother sent her from India last year," Bronwen told her, leaving once more.

"Turmeric?" Natasha and her mother echoed.

"Where are you going?" her mother added, as Bronwen pulled the bell chain and picked up her shawl.

"Out. There was angelica in the forest. Then, I must talk to the cook about borage and black current seed oil."

"What are you up to now?" Annalies demanded.

"If we must stay here until Christmas, then I must do something or go mad with the waiting. I can help Hr. Fisker, mother. I know I can. The turmeric is a particularly powerful antidote, although I can help him even before it arrives."

Annalies studied her. "Very well," she said. "What can I do to help?"

* * * * *

"What is it you read with such a deep frown, Baumgärtner?" Tor demanded. Normally he would not care. Now, though, he was desperate for any distraction. The view outside his window showed dreary, over-crowded streets of Brussels. Even the hostel they were quartered in was hip-deep with princes and dukes. The palace could not accommodate everyone who arrived in Brussels for the coronation. It was rumored even Queen Victoria was to be housed in the Magistrate's house. Although, she would have the home to herself, while mere dukes and princes must live cheek to jowl.

Baumgärtner was the only one of Tor's retinue given quarters near Tor. Everyone else from Silkeborg was located in an even more distant inn, three to a room.

Discussing news from home would lift the tedium of waiting for an event that had not yet been announced.

Baumgärtner shook his head and put the letter inside the leather portfolio where he kept his current documents. "Borgmester Østergård sings the praises of a mad Englishwoman visiting Silkeborg. A witch, he says, who has cured Magistrate Fisker of his aches, when the best doctors in the world could not." Baumgärtner snorted his derision. "Always, the Great English are praised for mere ordinary accomplishments, as if they might hear us and remember."

Tor grew still. "A witch?" His heart squeezed. "An English witch." He sank onto the bench under the window, his breath whooshing from him. "It cannot be…"

Baumgärtner tilted his head. "You know this woman?"

"I…might," Tor said cautiously. "Does Borgmester Østergård give her name?"

Baumgärtner opened his portfolio and read the letter. "A…Lady Coburg, he thinks. Or perhaps Lady…Davies? He is not certain, for Magistrate Fisker was quite excited when they spoke."

"Davies," Tor repeated. He leaned forward, threading his hands together to hide their sudden tremble. "*Miss* Davies." He remembered to breathe. "She is in *Silkeborg*," he whispered, stunned.

"*Miss* Davies?" Baumgärtner repeated. "A commoner?"

"You know her, Baumgärtner, so stop turning up your overly delicate nose. You met her in Yorkshire. Why would Fisker confuse her name that way? Unless...perhaps the Princess Annalies is with her. People are often confused by her mother." His mouth turned up. "Or so I've heard." For Bronwen had delighted in shocking him with tales about her royal mother with bluestocking blood.

"Her mother is a *princess*?" Baumgärtner said, his interest perking. "You met her in England? When? Where? Did you get along? Is she pleasing to the eye?"

Tor held up his hand. "Calm yourself. Bronwen would tell you herself she is not suitable duchess material. You can extinguish that glint of hope in your eyes. The lady would rather wander the dales of Northallerton than dine with dukes."

Baumgärtner looked affronted. Then he frowned again. "Wait, wait. Northallerton? She was *there*? Do you speak of that...that...*waif*? The one with the dirty hems?"

Tor leaned back. "The very one."

"Oh, dear." Baumgärtner let out a deep, bitter sigh. "Still, there is Lady Dagmar, who pines for your return to Silkeborg." Baumgärtner looked at him from under his brow. Perhaps he was trying to look coy. The expression did not suit a sixty-year-old man. "She was devastated when you disappeared in Scotland."

Tor thought of the far-too-slender woman with distaste.

"If only she could hold a conversation that lasted longer than two minutes."

Baumgärtner slapped the desk with the flat of his hand. "One day you must bring yourself to it, your Highness! Putting the duchy at risk in this way is intolerable!"

"I know, Aldous. I know." Tor sighed.

Baumgärtner opened his portfolio one more time. "I will write back to Borgmester Østergård and make further enquiries about this witch woman."

"You waste your time," Tor warned him. "She is a commoner."

"She is the daughter of a princess," Baumgärtner said primly.

"She will not consider it. I would not let her," Tor replied. "She would come to hate my life and everyone in it, even if she were mad enough to agree."

"She would be mad to refuse you. You are an Archeduke!"

"Her father is a bastard," Tor replied, slapping Baumgärtner with the bald, unpalatable truth.

Baumgärtner shook his head. "You have turned your back upon every princess Europe has to offer. A ragamuffin is all that is left. At least her blood is blue, which is more than can be said for certain about Lady Dagmar."

Tor couldn't help laughing. The puritanical downturn of Baumgärtner's mouth jolted him into it. "Write your letter, then. Determine for yourself that the Magistrate's witch is ninety years old and has no teeth left. Then you can marry her yourself."

Because it could not possibly be Bronwen in Silkeborg. It was impossible, a mere figment of his hope, which Baumgärtner would crush out of existence with the return mail.

Chapter Fourteen

Borgmester Østergård's coach was an open-topped one, of which he was overtly proud. He ordered the top be folded away while he toured Bronwen, Annalies, Natasha and Elisa about Silkeborg, showing them the little town and discussing his plans to build it into a great city.

As there were only four thousand people living in the town and there had never been more in the long history of the place, it was unlikely Silkeborg would ever grow enough to become a city. However, Bronwen held her tongue and shivered beneath the fur lap blanket.

Østergård was a tall man. Height seemed to be a national trait in Denmark. He was also thin, with sharp angular cheeks and dark circles beneath his eyes. His tall top hat made him look even taller. His mustache drooped at the corners as if it, too, wished to add to the illusion of extra height, instead of growing outward.

He pointed out the row of blacksmiths, the village square, the little artisan shops and the civil buildings, while Bronwen's mother and Natasha and Elisa looked suitably impressed.

Bronwen's attention was drawn by a tragic tableau of people sitting at the tables in front of the café, with steaming coffee cups in front of them. Of the five people at the table, three of them were bent and wizened. They sat in postures that spoke of suffering. No one was talking.

As if he had just spoken the words, Bronwen recalled Tor's voice telling her; My own country suffers. There is a sickness that has gripped it for years. People die. Healthy, young people. Old, frail people. Women, children, men. The sickness does not distinguish who it chooses as its next victim. It can strike anyone and every time the symptoms are different. No expert can tell me what the problem is.

Bronwen turned her head to study the listing people, as the coach passed. She looked back at Østergård.

"They are ill, yes?" she asked him.

"They are." He was barely audible above the clop of the horse.

"That is why you insisted upon taking us on this excursion, isn't it?"

He sat back. "You are most astute, Miss Davies. That was the hidden purpose for my invitation. Although I did indeed want to thank you for your kindness toward Magistrate Fisker and show you a little of our town."

Bronwen trembled. "How many are ill?"

"As of yesterday, apart from the usual sicknesses that visit themselves upon any town, anywhere in the world, Silkeborg has one hundred and fifty-seven people with mysterious symptoms that experts cannot diagnose. They are different, in different people."

"In a population this small, that is a significant number," Bronwen's mother said, from the other side of the coach.

"You think I can do what experts could not?" Bronwen asked, stunned.

Borgmester Østergård's smile was rueful. "What have I

got to lose?"

Bronwen shook her head. "My only expertise is that I have read widely. That is not a skill which can cure what ails your people, Borgmester."

"Still, I would ask that you try. You have an uncanny knack for coupling odd facts, or so I understand from your explanation of how you cured Magistrate Fisker."

"I did not cure him," Bronwen said tiredly. "I only relieved his symptoms. His disease cannot be cured."

"You gave him respite, when others could not. That is not insignificant."

Bronwen realized she was wringing her gloved hands together and made them stop. She put her hands beneath the fur once more and shuddered, this time with more than cold.

Elisa sat forward and touched her knee. "What would it hurt to try?" she asked reasonably. "The Borgmester is correct. You do have a gift for putting together stray facts. Perhaps you will stumble upon even part of the truth."

"You were looking for something to do, were you not?" her mother asked.

Bronwen sighed and looked at Østergård. "I can try," she said. "That is all I can promise."

"Very good. Very, *very* good," he said. He lifted his voice and called out to the driver, who cracked the whip. The horses picked up the pace.

"Where are we going?" Bronwen asked, as the coach turned out of the market square.

"To visit the ill and the dead," Østergård said. "While I

have your attention, I would use it wisely."

"May we have the top put up while we do so?" Bronwen asked.

"On a beautiful, warm day like today?" Borgmester Østergård protested.

* * * * *

After the seventh stop at a small, painted cottage, where the hapless owner and his family suffered, Bronwen trudged toward the carriage where her mother and Natasha and Elisa waited—with the top up, now. Borgmester Østergård walked alongside her, keeping pace with his much longer legs.

"The child was barely six years old," she whispered, distress making her eyes sting.

"Seven, although I'm told he will not see his eighth year," Østergård replied.

Bronwen stopped in the middle of the neat path, which had been scrupulously cleared of all snow and looked up at him. "I am not sure I can stand to see another, Borgmester Østergård. I am not able to help them. Their illnesses are unknown to me. I have never read of such an odd collection of complaints."

Borgmester Østergård nodded. "May I add one more to your tally, before you end the day? Then I will take you and the Princess and the two ladies to dine at my house."

"I suppose, yes, if I must." Bronwen tried to smile. "I'm afraid I have no appetite now."

"I understand," he replied. "I have not had much appetite for several years now."

Bronwen sighed. "And the last patient?"

"Me," he said.

Her heart sank. "Oh…"

"It is a growth, I am told. In here." He touched his belly. "Soon, it will halt the functioning of an important organ and then I will die. In the meantime, though, I work to save those people I can. This is my town, Miss Davies. I have lived here all my life. I have dined with the Archeduke many times…the previous Archeduke, I mean. I am a man of means, yet I am a victim. This malady that smites us is unjust and unfair, choosing the rich, the poor, the young, the old. I would rid Silkeborg of its menace before I die."

She stared at his middle, as if she might see the tumor he spoke of with her naked eye.

There was a word she had heard used in the more obscure medical texts that described Borgmester Østergård's condition. "Cancer," she murmured.

His brow lifted. "That is what one doctor called it."

"Cancer is not a mysterious illness," she pointed out. "It is very rare, although it is not mysterious. Doctors have known about it since Hippocrates' time."

"Then I am one of the rare people and it is just a coincidence that my illness struck me at the same moment this plague descended upon Silkeborg."

"Perhaps not. Coincidences can happen. They are rare in nature, though." She considered him, her thoughts swirling. "You said one hundred and fifty-seven people had mysterious symptoms, while others were sick with normal diseases. What are those diseases?"

"Consumption. Infections." He shrugged. "I am assured the numbers are normal for a population of this size."

"What if they are not?" she asked. "What if some of those normal illnesses are caused by the same source that causes the mysterious symptoms?" She stood with her head down, thinking.

Borgmester Østergård stayed silent.

There was something he had just said… She frowned, recalling what he had said, then lifted her head. "You said your illness came upon you at the same time everyone else grew ill. Did you mean that *everyone* who is ill, became so at the same moment?"

He shook his head and she sighed. "They have occurred across several years," he added.

Bronwen turned and headed for the coach once more. Then she halted again and spun to look at him. "The same several years? There was nothing before that? What years? When did it start?"

He frowned. "I would need to consult the charts the doctors compiled. The Archeduke insisted upon records being kept." He shook his head. "They are in the municipal offices, back in the square."

"Can we consult the charts? Now?" she asked.

"You are still not hungry?" he asked.

"Not until I've seen the charts. Please, Borgmester."

His smile was sad. "Very well. Others have studied them, without success. Although, we *are* clutching at straws…"

* * * * *

Borgmester Østergård translated her requests, while his clerks hurried, finding chairs for Annalies, Natasha and Elisa, who were more than happy to trail behind and observe. Another clerk, this one an older man with no hair, carried a big leather-bound notebook out from an inner office and placed it on the table in front of Bronwen and bowed. Talking quickly, he turned the heavy cover and flipped pages and pages of notes written in a variety of hands and inks, until he came to the last and tapped it.

Bronwen stepped forward. "Danish, of course," she said, looking at the page. She glanced up at Østergård. "What is this page?"

"This year's listings," Østergård said.

"I would like to see the first year's listings."

Østergård conveyed the request and the clerk closed the book with a thump, then opened it and stepped back, bowing again.

Bronwen looked at the first page.

"Shall I translate?" Østergård asked.

She shook her head. "A date is a date in any language." She ran her finger across an entry and spotted it. "Eighteen fifty-eight. Eight years ago." She looked at Østergård. "What happened in Silkeborg eight years ago?"

"Others asked that same question." He shook his head. "The answer is, nothing. Nothing of significance happened."

Bronwen looked down at the cramped handwriting on the first page. "Nothing you know of," she murmured. "Diseases like cancer have long periods of silent growth. Years. Consumption can take years to be noticed. The mystery symptoms may have similar diseases at their base that also take years to develop. What has happened in Silkeborg of any significance in the ten years before that?"

Østergård frowned.

"You have lived here all your life," Bronwen pointed out. "What events do you remember?"

He laughed. "The only event of significance in the last one hundred years, apart from the deaths of three Archedukes, has been the opening of the paper mill."

Annalies gasped and got to her feet. "There is a paper mill here?" she asked, moving up to the table.

"A modern one," Borgmester Østergård said, pride back in his voice. "It is located on the river, just around the bend from the town. I planned to take you there to visit, only my excursion was interrupted." His smile was as small and gentle as his teasing.

Annalies looked at Bronwen. "If it is a new mill, then it most likely uses chlorine to whiten the pulp." She glanced at Borgmester Østergård. "I read about it," she explained.

Borgmester Østergård nodded. "I, too, read about the processes. We considered the mill, your Highness. Only, it is not workers at the mill who grow ill. It is anyone in the village, or just outside it. It cannot be the mill that is at fault, for it was here for years before the illnesses began."

"How many years?" Bronwen asked. "When was it built?"

"Eighteen fifty-five."

Bronwen stared through the tall man, thinking. Eighteen fifty-five was three years before any symptoms had appeared in the town.

Annalies bit her lip. "Why would villagers fall ill and not mill workers?"

"Not *just* mill-workers," Bronwen replied.

"I fear you are following a false lead, your Highness, Miss Davies," Østergård told them. "The mill is *not* the source."

Bronwen put her face in her hands. *Something* niggled in her mind, something that had looked normal, yet was not. Something she *should* have noticed.

"Deductive. Inductive. *What?*" she whispered.

Someone came into the office, sending a cold blast of air across the room, drawing attention to the heat the potbellied stoves were belching out.

"The cold!" Bronwen said, lifting her face from her hands.

Annalies nodded. "What about it?"

"The river wasn't frozen." Bronwen gripped her mother's sleeve. "It's *cold* and the river wasn't frozen." She turned to Borgmester Østergård. "When was the last time the river froze in winter?"

Borgmester Østergård was no longer smiling. "That is not a record we keep."

"Ask him," Bronwen said, nodding at the older clerk,

who was standing politely, unable to follow their English. "As your memory is failing."

"Bronwen…" her mother breathed in warning.

"Please," Bronwen added, giving Østergård her best smile.

Borgmester Østergård considered her for a long, silent moment. Then he turned to the clerk and rattled out a question in Danish.

The clerk frowned, thinking. Then he spoke, glancing at Bronwen and her mother.

"What did he say?" Bronwen pressed Østergård.

"He said it has been over ten years since they got to skate on the river at Christmas. Before that, the river froze every winter." Østergård fished out his watch and consulted it. "I must return you to the Magistrate's house. I have an appointment. This way, please."

"But—" Bronwen began, as he attempted to shepherd them through the door.

"I am running very late, I am so sorry," Østergård insisted.

"There is direct empirical evidence—" Bronwen began.

"Not now," her mother whispered and guided her toward the door.

Bronwen let herself be led out to the waiting coach and bundled inside. Østergård shut the door on them and peered through the door. "I bid you goodnight, ladies. Axelson will see you home." He touched his brim and turned away.

The coach moved forward with a jolt, rattling the four of them.

"I don't understand," Bronwen said, looking at the other three. "It is *clearly* the paper mill that is the source of the problem. Mother, mills use a lot of water, yes? That's why they are always on rivers or lakes."

"Yes," Annalies admitted.

"And the river hasn't frozen since the mill was built," Bronwen concluded. "They're putting something in the water. Maybe even the chlorine you mentioned. I don't know the chemistry for that—"

"It is an acid. A powerful one," Annalies replied.

"If something like that was in the town's water, then that is why everyone is falling ill. Borgmester Østergård could see that was what I was about to say, so why did he cut me off?"

"I think you're missing a vital point," Natasha said. It was the first time she had spoken for a long while, although her interest in the investigation had been no less than Bronwen's.

"What would the point be, Natasha?" Elisa asked, with a tone that said she expected to be surprised.

"Politics," Natasha replied.

Annalies leaned back. "Or economics, depending upon how one considers it."

"In a town this size, politics and economics are blood brothers," Elisa added.

Bronwen gripped a fold of her dress. "Borgmester Østergård does not want to know the truth because he fears he will lose his post as Borgmester?" She shook her head. "He cares about the town too much and besides, he's dying." She sat up. "No, it is more basic than that. The mill likely employs dozens...*hundreds* of people." She looked at the three older ladies. "He is afraid that if the mill is the source and it is shut down, *everyone* will suffer, not just those who are ill. He is protecting his town."

The coach came to a halt. Now that Borgmester Østergård was not a passenger, the driver did not seem to care about throwing his passengers around with sharp stops and starts.

Bronwen sat back upon the seat and looked through the window. There were two tall figures standing on the narrow balcony at the front of the Magistrate's house. "Why, that is Benjamin, isn't it?"

Annalies ducked to look through the window, too. "And Wakefield!"

Sharla hurried out onto the balcony and waved at them. "I brought your turmeric!" she called.

"I asked that she *send* it," Bronwen breathed, stunned. She looked at Elisa.

Elisa shrugged. "I may have stressed the urgency a tad."

The driver did not climb from his bench to open the door for them, so Ben leapt down the stairs to the road and opened it, instead. He helped them out while Sharla hugged them one at a time and Dane bowed over each of their hands.

When Bronwen held her hand out to step down, Ben's dropped away as he studied her. "Oh my lord!" he breathed.

"That's not what you say to a lady, idiot," Dane said, coming forward. He held out his hand. "Although Ben has just cause. You are a most delightful and beautiful version of your former self." He bent over her hand, not quite kissing it. His gaze met hers. His eyes twinkled. "Do I detect a man at the root of this great change?"

Bronwen pulled her hand from his, trying not to rise in response to his accurate teasing. "Dane, Ben, Sharla, there was no need for you to rush to Belgium for the sake of a pound of turmeric," she told them. "Though it is very good to see you."

"A pound of turmeric and this," Dane said, digging in his coat. He pulled out a letter with a flourish and presented it to Annalies. "The same coat of arms is on the front as was on mine. You, your Highness, have been invited to attend the coronation of King Leopold the Second, in Brussels, on the seventeenth of this month."

"That's three days from now," Sharla added. "That's why we brought it ourselves. Dane didn't want to use even a private courier and risk you missing the letter and slighting the new King."

Dane waved toward the coach. "We have a special waiting at the train station. How fast can you pack your trunks?"

"It only takes a few hours to reach Belgium from here," Annalies pointed out.

Natasha shook her head. "A coronation is usually accompanied by a ball. That's why Sharla looks so pleased."

Sharla's smile widened. "Paris is a day away. That leaves a day to buy a ball gown and I want to visit the House of Worth to buy mine."

Chapter Fifteen

"He can't be here," Jack said. "Even if he is then how, in God's good graces, are we supposed to find him?"

Will stepped around a trio of Irish Wolfhounds being escorted by leash through the narrow aisle. He readjusted his coat and brushed it to rid it of coarse dog hair. "I tell you, he's here. Travers was certain. Cian left the townhouse this morning after breakfast, the same as always and said he was coming to the show."

Jack stepped over to the side of the busy aisle, moving out of the tide of men, dogs and even a pig or two and looked around helplessly. The huge hall had a domed roof that soared to ninety feet at the top of the peak. Because the hall was longer than it was wide, the ridge ran for more than a hundred yards. The hall should have been airy and fresh because of it, however, every spare inch was fenced off into tiny paddocks. Each enclosure was strewn with calf-deep hay and each enclosure held a staggering array of bulls, cows, sheep, pigs. All of them were bellowing, snorting, bleating and squealing. Exotic chickens, with spots and colorful tails, added to the din.

Hay dust floated in the air above the heads of the thousands of people squashed into the narrow aisles between the display pens. The stench was unbelievable. If the roof had been any lower, the aroma would have been intolerable.

"Why didn't Cian send that new estate manager of his here? Why come himself?" Jack demanded, as Will waved his hand in front of his nose.

Will shrugged. "Because it's what he's always done?" He scratched at his beard. "It's Cian. He's always been a law unto himself. Let's divide up the place. An aisle each. Up and back, then meet back here at the top. It'll go faster. I have an appointment in the city at two." He pulled out his watch and flipped the lid, then frowned.

Jack shook his head. "I have a better idea. Look." He pointed into the air, high over their heads. A large board hung from chains. Painted on it in gold and white lettering was the announcement, "Dining Saloon," with a hand pointing to the left.

Will saw what he was looking at. "Brandy," he said and clapped Jack's shoulder. "I do believe you're right. Let's start there."

They eased their way through the aisle to where the entrance to the dining room cut through the pens and punched through the side of the hall. Beyond was the soaring roof of yet another hall, although no hay dust floated in the air.

They stepped through into the far quieter, smaller hall and Will sighed and patted his coat, then readjusted the sit of his hat. "This is better."

There were dozens of small tables, each with a white tablecloth, condiments and cutlery. As it was nearly noon, many of the tables had occupants. Waiters with white aprons scurried between the table, bringing trays of meals from the kitchen on the far side. There were few women in the hall. Most of them were vigorously waving their fans to disperse the rich aromas in the air.

There was also a bar on the other side. Jack slapped Will's arm. "There he is."

"As close to the brandy decanter as he can get," Will confirmed.

They walked around the tables and up to the bar. Cian stood at the bar, his hat next to him, a nearly empty glass in front of him. He was the tallest man at the bar, although his height was not apparent because he had his head bent, reading.

Jack and Will walked right up to him before he noticed them. He looked up, his clear eyes narrowing. "What are you doing here?"

"And good morning to you, too," Jack said.

Will cleared his throat. "We heard the news, Cian."

Cian didn't react.

"About the storm off the Dubh Artach reef in Scotland," Jack added. Alarmed, he added, "You know about it, don't you? It has been in the papers the last two days now…"

"Twenty-four ships lost at sea," Cian said crisply. "Yes, I read about it." He folded up the letter he was reading. Before the content was hidden, Jack saw the letterhead.

His alarm increased. "That's a letter from Eleanore?" he asked.

"As it happens, yes." Cian picked up the glass and swallowed the large mouthful that remained, then dumped the glass back on the bar with a loud knock. He shoved the letter into his inner pocket, crumpling it. "It was in this morning's mail. All the way from Skye in only five days. The modern mail system is an absolute marvel, is it not?"

He picked up his hat and walked swiftly along the side of the hall, heading for the exit doors at the end.

Jack looked at Will. Will shook his head, frowning.

Both of them hurried after Cian, jogging to catch him.

"They're reporting Gainsford as one of the passengers lost," Jack said. "Was Eleanore on the *Highland Queen* with her father? Was she coming back to London for Christmas, too?"

"That is what her letter says," Cian said, his tone crisp. He didn't stop walking.

Will caught Jack's eye again. Jack could see the worry in his glance.

Jack caught at Cian's arm. "Wait, Cian. Stop, just for one moment, will you?"

"Can't, sorry. Things to do." He shrugged off Jack's grip, not missing a step. He moved around a group of people standing right in the middle of the exit with a long side step. Jack and Will bobbed around the group, muttered apologies and hurried out into the crisp air, following him.

Cian was still walking, now heading for busy Upper Street, where the usual long line of private carriages stood waiting for their owners to return. Beyond the clogged thoroughfare was Islington Green, the grass a dull brown now the snow had melted.

Jack and Will caught up with him again.

"Cian," Jack began once more. "Talk to us."

Cian still did not stop.

Will swore and took a huge step around Cian, putting himself in the way so Cian could not progress without either moving around him or pushing him.

Cian tried to step around him. Jack put himself in the way and grabbed his arm. "No you don't."

"Talk, Cian. I want to know you are not…" Will began.

"Deranged?" Cian asked him, his voice flat. "Out of my mind with secret grief?"

Jack didn't like the empty expression in Cian's eyes. "You know she's likely dead, Cian?"

Cian's gaze swiveled to him. "Of course she is dead."

Jack swayed back, shocked by his flat, certain tone.

"It's not as sure a thing as that," Will said. "They're still fishing people out of the sea…" He trailed off, as uncomfortable with Cian's lack of reaction as Jack.

"Oh, she *is* dead," Cian told him. His high cheek bones seemed stark, his cheeks thin and drawn. The glassy look in his eyes matched the bleak expression. "It's better this way."

"What in hell, Cian?" Jack ejected, stunned.

Cian shrugged. "It's better she is dead and completely out of my reach, than married and dangling there where I can see her every day."

Jack gasped, sick pain spearing him, as a memory of Jenny's pale face under her wedding veil came to him.

Will gripped Jack's arm. "He doesn't mean it that way,

Jack. He doesn't know what he's saying right now," he said softly and urgently.

Jack let out another shuddering breath. "Let him go drown his sorrows by himself. He doesn't need us. I shouldn't have bothered rushing down from Lincolnshire. Let him go."

Cian looked at Will's hand, still holding his sleeve. "You heard the man. Do you mind?"

Will let his sleeve go and stepped back. "Jack's right. You're a cold, heartless bastard."

"Thank you." Cian moved through the two of them, shouldering Jack aside. He walked on and Jack turned to watch him leave, unable to believe the callousness Cian had just shown.

The new cabriolet Cian had purchased to travel about the city was standing by the curb. Cian strode toward it, digging in his coat. He withdrew the letter he had been reading at the bar and unfolded it as he walked.

Only, he didn't stop at the cab. He moved around it, his head down, reading the letter. Then he walked between his cab and the nose of the horse behind it, still reading. A yard beyond the cab, the heavy traffic of Upper Street clattered.

"God in his heaven…" Will breathed.

Jack ran, an all-out sprint that was better than any time he'd ever made at Cambridge. Will, who was usually faster, could only keep pace.

Cian walked out onto Upper Street, as if he was strolling Rotten Row.

The driver of a carriage yelled and hauled on his reins,

making the horse neigh and his hooves skid on the cobbles.

Cian didn't react. Instead, he took another few steps and came to a halt, head down, still reading. He stood in the far lane of traffic. Coming from the south was a charabanc and pair. The driver yelled and stood on the brake, as the passengers screamed.

Jack didn't know how he made it. He remembered nothing of his sprint and lunge across the street. He could only see Cian, standing in the middle of the street. He dove, his arm out, and took Cian right off his feet.

They rolled three or four times and came to a stop on cobbles. They were still on the street. Jack cringed.

Will gripped the shoulder of his coat and hauled. Cian slid along with him. Will was dragging both of them. Jack could hear him grunting with the effort.

The gutter was filthy. Jack didn't care. He rolled over it, onto the footpath beyond, breathing hard, then lifted himself up to examine Cian.

Cian lay on the pavement, staring up at the sky. It was as if nothing had happened. His face was placid. His lips moved as if he was speaking.

Jack shook him. "Cian!"

Will bent over the two of them, breathing hard. "Bloody hell!" he muttered.

People were gathering around them, exclaiming and jabbering.

Jack bent close to listen to Cian's whispers.

"She was never mine. Now, she will never be anyone's…"

Jack sighed. He looked up at Will. "You may have to miss your appointment."

Will nodded, his eyes grave.

* * * * *

The carriage was roomy enough for six people. Dane paid the driver a large tip to nudge as close to the cathedral as possible. It would give them the best view of the entrance, where attendees to the coronation were gathering. After Dane and Annalies had exited the carriage and joined the mass of attendees moving into the cathedral, there were five of them left to huddle beneath the lap robes and watch the procession.

Sharla, who was wearing a new day dress, had been disappointed to learn she must remain in the carriage.

"Invitations to a coronation are about title and rank," Elisa told her. "Even Dane will have to stand at the far back of the cathedral. He may see nothing of the coronation itself. To fail to attend, though, would be an insult the royal family would remember."

"The ball tonight is a different matter," Natasha added, sipping her mulled wine. Steam rose from the cup. "Dane and Annalies were both invited. The invitation includes 'friends'. That means all of us may attend."

Ben put his arm around Sharla and pulled her against him and rubbed her arms to warm her. "You'll get to show me and Dane your pretty ball gown, yet," he told her.

Sharla wrinkled her nose. "Perhaps I didn't buy a new

gown."

Ben laughed. "You'll still be the most beautiful woman there, even in an old gown." He kissed her cheek.

"The coronation is about ceremony," Natasha said, as Elisa smiled at the pair. Natasha's gaze met Bronwen's. "The ball is about politics. That's why the invitations are loosely phrased. Everyone is interested in currying favor with the new king."

"And because the balance of power in Europe has shifted around the new King, everyone else will shore allegiances and form new ones," Bronwen finished.

Natasha said, with a small smile, "People expect upsets at times like this."

Bronwen peered through the window at the thinning crowd around the steps of the cathedral. Footmen were trying to guide them up the steps. "It will start soon," she said.

"Tall, blond, clean shaven…is that him there, Bronwen?" Elisa asked, tapping the window. "Over by the far doors. He's by himself."

Bronwen shifted her gaze, looking for a lone man.

Tor was climbing the steps, his gaze ahead. She studied him hungrily. Was it her imagination, or had he lost weight? His hair was the same thick thatch, only trimmed and brushed into order now, instead of whipped about by the wind and hanging over his forehead and shadowing his blue eyes.

He was wearing a formal military uniform, one that Bronwen had never before seen. The great coat was light blue, with red braid curling and swirling up the sleeve and across the chest. The tunic beneath was also blue, with a red, high collar and gold buttons.

Then someone moved ahead and she saw him from head to toe. His uniform trousers were blue, too, with red stripes up the side. He held a gold helmet beneath his arm. Feathers waved from the top of it.

As the Archeduke of Silkeborg, Tor was by birthright one of the most senior generals of the Danish kingdom's army. Bronwen had read about the Danish monarchy, more than once. Now it was a solid reality, with personal meaning.

He was once more the man she didn't know. "He looks so different," she whispered.

"When he kisses you, he won't be," Sharla whispered.

Bronwen looked over her shoulder at Sharla. "*If* he kisses me."

"Oh, he'll kiss you," Ben said, his tone warm.

Sharla slapped his arm.

Ben pulled her back against him. "If the man has an ounce of warm blood in him, he'll take one glance at Bronwen in her new finery and he won't be able to help himself."

"That's even worse, Ben!" Sharla told him.

"If I were you, I would stop speaking at once," Natasha told him.

"No, let him hang himself properly," Sharla muttered, her eyes narrowed.

Bronwen brushed the bodice of her golden brown velvet walking suit self-consciously, watching Tor as he disappeared through the big cathedral doors.

"I only mean," Ben continued, "that *other* men might feel

that way. I, however, look at Bronwen and all I see is her doing cartwheels on the croquet court, her skirt over her ears and her bare feet and muddy ankles waving."

Bronwen saw a familiar figure on the far side of the cathedral, standing next to a rented carriage of the same size as theirs. Baumgärtner, Tor's secretary. The old man watched the last of the dignitaries move inside the cathedral, then stepped up into the carriage. Through the carriage's window, Bronwen could see the blonde woman sitting, staring at the cathedral as Bronwen had just been doing. She wore a fur hat and jewels at her ears. Her dress was also trimmed with pale fur.

She was every inch a lady.

Bronwen sighed. "What if Tor is like Ben?" she asked everyone in the carriage. "What if he looks at me and all he sees is the woman he met in Yorkshire?"

Chapter Sixteen

"Now turn slowly, so I can see every inch," Sharla instructed.

Bronwen drew in a shaking breath and turned, as Sharla, Natasha, Elisa and her mother critiqued her dress and appointments with a critical eye.

"This reminds me of your coming out, Sharla," Elisa said with a soft smile.

"Yes, I was just thinking the same thing," Sharla admitted. "Stop, Bronwen! There is a loop of Illusion hanging where it should not. Do you see that, Aunt Natasha?"

"Yes, I do." Natasha came forward, a needle and thread in her hands and bent to tuck the offending netting back into place and stitch it.

Bronwen pressed her hand against her belly, feeling the nervous flutter there as she had all afternoon while Sharla, her mother, Aunt Natasha and Aunt Elisa prepared her for the ball, while debating how best to present her.

Their own toilets had been swift and minimal. They were practiced at the art of beauty, while Bronwen was still stumbling through the simplest ways to move her hoops through narrow doorways and not reveal her ankles. Consequently, the four women were dressed in their elegant ballgowns long before they had finished with Bronwen's.

The gown was a House of Worth creation, as was Sharla's mauve and blue silk. Sharla had directed the choosing of

Bronwen's gown. It had been Sharla who had spotted the dull brown dress among the purples and greens and vibrant blues and rainbow hues clustered in the viewing lounge.

"It's brown," Bronwen said. "I thought I was supposed to stop wearing mud."

"It's *gold*," Sharla corrected her. "Also, it is silk. In here, with this poor light, it doesn't show well. In a ballroom, with the lights and against your skin and hair, it will be the perfect complement."

Natasha spread the skirt of the dress out for inspection. It was very full. "Perhaps Sharla is right."

"At least try it on," Elisa urged. "A dress never looks like much until the undergarments are supporting it."

"It seems plain," Bronwen said.

"On our way back to the hotel, we will buy fifteen yards of Illusion," Sharla told her. "You won't walk into the ballroom, Bronwen. You will *float*."

The dress had been fitted for her, although there had been little adjustment necessary. The Illusion had been purchased and Sharla had spent two hours arranging the fine netting and draping it about the dress, a fine pucker on her brow as she concentrated.

Now the four of them were standing around her as Bronwen turned, examining every inch.

"When can I look in a mirror?" Bronwen asked one more time.

"Soon," Sharla said absently. "That eighteen-inch waist of yours is divine, Bronwen. If walking is the cause, I will start walking for miles every day, immediately."

"The corset is rather tight," Bronwen said apologetically.

"It is comfortably tight," Elisa said. "Any tighter and you could not dance. I brought it in just enough to fit the dress and that is all. When you are not expecting to dance, you might be able to bring it in another inch or two."

"While I seem to have to let mine out every week," Sharla muttered.

Elisa gasped and spun to face her. "You do?"

Natasha lifted her chin with a shocked expression.

Annalies just smiled, holding her gloved hands together against her chin in delight.

Elisa skirted around Bronwen's dress and confronted Sharla, who looked confused and a little frightened. "Shh…" Elisa said, patting her cheek. "Don't you know? You didn't suspect?"

"Suspect?" Sharla breathed.

"Your doctor will confirm for you, although a woman's corset is a more reliable marker," Natasha said.

"I am almost completely certain you are with child, my dear," Elisa told Sharla.

Sharla drew in a sharp breath. Her eyes glittered. She fumbled for her top hoop. "I must…I must speak to Ben and Dane…" She hurried away.

Natasha stood up, her stitching finished. She tucked the needle back in the box, then slid on her own long gloves. "You may look in the mirror now," she told Bronwen.

Annalies and Elisa stepped back out of the way and Bronwen moved over to where the big, three-paned mirror stood in the corner. She held her breath and stepped to where she could see herself.

Sharla had been right to insist upon this dress. It wasn't an exact match with her hair, but a lighter shade of the same hue. The silk glowed in the candlelight in the dressing room, making it resemble old gold, glinting softly.

She had never worn hoops this wide. She had never *seen* hoops this big. From her waist, which seemed to be smaller than ever, the gold skirt spread about her, making it impossible to let her hands hang by her sides. Behind her, the hem of the skirt extended into a short train. The edge of the skirt was finished with tiny box pleats, each sewn with golden beads.

From midway down the skirt to the floor, hung garlands of Illusion, each caught up and knotted to resemble a rose. The dress revealed her shoulders and more Illusion draped from the bodice.

The gold filigree necklace had five amethysts mounted along the front, sitting at the top of her breasts.

The only place where the Illusion did not soften the golden silk was at her waist.

"It is better to be able to see your waist clearly," Natasha had pointed out earlier that afternoon.

"And to be able hold it," Sharla had added, as she draped the Illusion. "For waltzes," she said hastily, when Annalies stared at her.

The sprays of tiny flowers in Bronwen's hair were the same color as the amethysts and they seemed to make her eyes appear blue, instead of gray.

Bronwen stared at herself, not quite believing the transformation.

Her mother stepped up behind her and met her eyes in the mirror. "You're in his world now, my darling."

"Yes," Bronwen agreed. Her voice shook.

"Remember, you belong here, too," Annalies whispered. "You've merely taken your rightful place, instead of choosing to live beyond its borders."

"I must keep reminding myself of that."

Annalies held out Bronwen's gloves. "Ready?"

Bronwen shook her head. "Why does this take more courage than walking away from society?"

"Because the prize is much bigger." Annalies dropped her cape around her shoulders and Bronwen buttoned it at the neck. She bent and kissed Bronwen's cheek. "No matter what happens, you are still my daughter and I am very proud of you."

"Thank you, Mama."

They moved out to the sitting room of the hotel suite. Sharla was already there with Ben and Dane. Her head was against Ben's shoulder, while Dane held both of them. It was a private moment and the three of them hastily separated as the women moved into the sitting room. Sharla wiped her eyes and sniffed.

Dane saw Bronwen and smiled. Then he put his heels together and bowed, his formal tails lifting behind him. "Miss Davies."

Ben laughed. "I think I feel sorry for the man. I know what it's like to watch beauty sway toward you and wonder what she is thinking."

Sharla smiled at him. "Mother, we—Dane and Ben and I—will only stay at the ball for an hour. I hope you don't mind?"

Elisa frowned. "There's no reason not to stay longer," she pointed out.

Dane shook his head. "Tomorrow, every train, every boat and every private conveyance will be commissioned to take everyone here for the coronation back home. We want to leave tonight. There is a train to Antwerp leaving at midnight and a boat to Gravesend tomorrow at noon. We want to return to London as soon as possible."

"I thought we could travel together," Elisa said.

"We want..." Dane began. He hesitated. "I hope you don't mind, only..."

"I want to tell Father," Ben said, looking at Annalies. "As soon as possible."

Bronwen's heart gave a little squeeze and hurried along.

Her mother's eyes glittered. "Yes," she said softy. "Yes, that would be the best Christmas present for him." She hugged Ben and kissed him, then Sharla and Dane in turn.

Then Annalies turned and faced everyone. "I believe it is time to leave. The ball will be starting."

* * * * *

When Bronwen saw the palace ahead, blazing with lights and with hundreds of coaches and carriages milling in front of the magnificent building, she shook in earnest.

Her mother picked up her hand. "You may not spot him

there straight away, remember," she murmured. "This is not his ball and there are many people here. Try to enjoy yourself, whether you see him or not."

"I will see him," Bronwen replied. "I know I will."

It took long moments for their coach to ease between departing and arriving vehicles, to get close enough to the front entrance of the palace for the footmen to open the door and hand them out. The delay only heightened Bronwen's nervousness.

By the time they were collected together upon the carpet, the ball was well underway. They could hear music coming from inside and the steady low murmur of conversations.

Dane held out both of his arms. "Sharla. Lady Elisa."

Ben held out his. "Mother. Aunt Natasha." He looked at Bronwen. "You should walk ahead of us."

Bronwen clutched at her bodice. "No!"

Annalies looked at her and raised her brow.

Reluctantly, Bronwen moved in front of them and stepped up the two steps into the front hall of the palace. Over the heads of the attendees in front of her, she could see a series of arches, with red swags pulled to either side, inside their graceful curves. Beyond the arches, a room blazed with the light from dozens of chandeliers. The music came from that room.

Another footman took her cape, leaving Bronwen exposed, visible to everyone. She shivered.

"Go on," Dane encouraged her, from behind.

Sharla pressed her fingers into the small of Bronwen's

back. "He won't be there. He's probably in a smoking room, drinking brandy. Go on."

The sound of people dancing beneath the chandeliers was louder now. So was the music.

People were turning to look at her. Their expressions were speculative. Were they wondering who she was?

Their stares were unsettling and pushed her into taking another few steps forward, then easing around groups of people, making her way deeper into the ballroom.

The light brightened. In the way that a crowded room could ebb and flow like currents in a river, the people before her separated. She could at last see the ballroom itself, the circle of dancers on the beautiful parquet floor and the people edging the big room, watching the dancers.

Then people shifted, moved to speak to others or for a clearer look at the dancers and her view was blocked once more. Bronwen turned to face Dane, Sharla and her mother. "He's not here," she said, relief letting her breathe. "I couldn't see him."

Annalies was staring over her shoulder. Then she reached and turned Bronwen's shoulders, making her spin around.

Tor *was* there. He stood on the edge of the dance floor, staring at her. He wore the same regal uniform he had been wearing at the coronation, although the great coat was gone and so was the helmet. The front of his tunic was covered in braid and medals and ribbons. His shoulders seemed wider than ever.

He came closer to them. His gaze did not lift away from

Bronwen.

She froze, all thought, all sense evaporating. She could only watch him, her heart racing wildly.

Dane and Sharla, Ben and Natasha and Elisa bowed and curtsied. Only Annalies, who was of higher rank, stood upright.

Belatedly, Bronwen realized she must do the same. She sank down. Tor held out his hand. "No," he said quickly.

She rose again, uncertainty gripping her.

Tor stepped closer. "It *is* you, isn't it? You're really here…" His blue eyes moved over her face.

Bronwen swallowed. "I know I look odd," she began. Behind her, Sharla gave an exasperated sound.

Tor let out a heavy breath. "Dance with me." He picked up her hand and without waiting for Bronwen to agree or not, led her out onto the floor.

Dancing was one society custom that Bronwen had never disagreed with. The dance was a sedate minuet which was just as well, for Tor did not seem to be able to look away from her and Bronwen could barely concentrate on the steps.

They came together, their hands raised. His eyes met hers.

Then apart.

The elegant circles were simple walking steps.

"I always find quieter rooms at these things," Tor said.

"For the brandy?"

"For the peace and quiet," he replied. "Tonight though, I just didn't want to. It was as if I was waiting for you."

Bronwen shuddered and turned away, following her own circle around and back to face him, as the other female dancers were doing.

"I heard there was an Englishwoman in Silkeborg," Tor said. "They said she was a witch. Was it you?"

Bronwen gasped. "Oh! Tor! I almost forgot in all the fuss…" She put her hand on his chest, for emphasis. "I found out what is wrong with the town! Why the people are sick! It was simple deductive reasoning. Inductive testing will prove I'm right, that it really is the paper mill that is at fault, only Borgmester Østergård will resist the truth because he is afraid the mill will have to close and that will be the end of the town…what are you doing?"

Tor cupped her cheek. He was smiling. "*There* you are. There's the woman from Yorkshire."

He kissed her, stealing her breath and making her thoughts drowsy. She realized with a start they were standing in the middle of the dance floor, forcing dancers to move around them, and that Tor was publicly kissing her.

She gasped as he let her go and gripped the braid on his tunic and shook him. "Are you listening to me?" she demanded. "The *paper mill* is the problem! They're putting something in the water."

He gripped her wrists. "I'm listening," he said. "Only, you must listen to me for a moment."

Bronwen glanced around the room. "We should remove ourselves from the dance floor."

"Hang them all," Tor said roughly. He shook her wrists. "I didn't come here tonight to dance with pretty ladies and trip over the most stunning beauty to ever cross my path."

With a start, Bronwen realized he was speaking of her. Her cheeks heated.

"I must speak to people," he continued, his voice low and urgent. "There are men here from far countries, people whom I will not have a chance to speak with again, if I do not grasp this chance. I must drink brandy and mingle... Why do you smile that way?"

"Politics," Bronwen said. "You must shore up your allies and friendships."

"Yes," he breathed. "*Yes*. You understand."

"I do." She pulled her hands from his fingers. "You should go."

"Not yet. Not before I know I will find you later, or tomorrow. Where are you staying?"

"The *Centralt*," she said. "Only, Tor, I want to leave early tonight to say farewell to my cousin. She and her husband and their...they are returning to England on the midnight train."

"Meet me tomorrow," he said, his tone still urgent. "Promise me."

Her heart swelled to bursting. "Yes."

His hand curled around the back of her neck, his fingertips making her skin tingle. He bent and kissed her once more. "Tomorrow," he breathed against her cheek. Then he stepped back two paces and bowed low. His eyes were heated as he lifted his head once more. Then he turned and threaded his way through the dancers.

Bronwen watched until she could see him no more.

Then she noticed the blond woman standing on the edge of the dancers, staring at Bronwen with an angry, bitter expression.

The woman in blue velvet.

Bronwen smiled at her, then went to find her family.

* * * * *

Annalies looked up from buttoning her own long coat over her day dress to run her gaze over Bronwen's velvet walking suit and the short cape that matched it. She nodded. "Ready?"

"Are you sure you should come, too, Mother?" Bronwen asked. "He did not say anything about a companion."

"You must trust me, darling daughter. You are not attending a social affair this morning. This is a negotiation and I will be there to represent you and protect your interests."

"Negotiation for what?" Bronwen felt her lip curl down. "Me?"

Annalies patted her cheek. "You won *that* particular negotiation last night. I suspect your Archeduke must now convince his advisors."

"Have I won?" Bronwen replied. "He has not asked me...anything. He has not said he loves me."

"He will not, not until he is sure enough to stand by the implied promise such confessions make." Annalies picked up her reticule and patted her hair.

"Fingertips, mother, remember?" Bronwen told her.

"Oh yes, thank you." She slid the locks back into place

and smiled at her. "Shall we?"

They moved out into the sitting room, where Natasha and Elisa were seated upon upright chairs, facing a third chair that Tor used. He got to his feet when Bronwen and her mother entered. He was wearing the plain black, elegant suit he had been wearing in Yorkshire. The military dress was gone.

His gaze drifted over Bronwen. His mouth turned up at the corner. "You look utterly delightful, Miss Davies."

"Bronwen," she insisted.

Tor bowed toward Annalies. "Princess Annalies, it is a pleasure. I have heard much about you."

"The edification has been mutual, Edvard."

"Please, call me Tor."

Annalies shook her head. "Not yet."

"Then, you are accompanying your daughter this morning?"

"Yes."

Tor smiled. "Good. Very good. Yes. The carriage is waiting." He bowed to Natasha and Elisa. "Ladies."

They curtsied.

Natasha waved to Bronwen, her smile warm.

* * * * *

The carriage ride took mere minutes, for the streets of Brussels had emptied as suddenly as a tipped glass. Tor did not speak and for most of the journey he looked out the window, as if his mind was elsewhere.

His distance did not reassure Bronwen.

Their destination was a large, traditional inn, with empty corridors and silent rooms. Tor showed them into a private lounge. "Please wait here a moment, while I find my secretary."

"Baumgärtner?" Bronwen asked.

"Yes." His gaze met hers. "There is business we must deal with before…well, let us finish business, first."

When he had shut the door, Annalies picked up her hand. "What comes next you may not enjoy, my darling. There will be harsh truths spoken—"

"I am not afraid of the truth," Bronwen replied.

"You may resent being discussed in ways that make you feel uncomfortable," her mother told her. "Remember that the only reason the discussion is being conducted is because the Archeduke wants the discussion, that he is forcing hands over you."

Bronwen shuddered. "Is this the way marriage is arranged with your people?"

Her mother smiled. "Now you know why I ran away and married your father." Annalies shook her hand. "Remember you are my daughter." She let her hand go as the door opened.

Baumgärtner followed Tor into the room. He was older and frailer than Bronwen remembered. He stopped short when he saw her and Annalies and took off his spectacles. "Well, my…" He coughed and replaced the spectacles.

"Your Highness," Tor said, "may I present to you my secretary and trusted advisor, Herr Aldous Baumgärtner?

Baumgärtner, this is the Princess Annalies Benedickta Davies, daughter of the royal house Saxe-Coburg-Weiden and of the former Principality of Saxe-Weiden."

Baumgärtner bowed low, his pointed beard jutting. "Your Highness."

Annalies inclined her head. "Baumgärtner."

"And this is Miss Bronwen Davies, the Princess' daughter, whom you may remember from Yorkshire."

"Indeed," Baumgärtner said, taking her hand and bowing over it. "You are…changed, Miss Davies."

"The change is purely superficial, I assure you," Bronwen said. Her eyes widened at her own temerity. What had made her say that? "I mean," she added hastily, "It is only polite to adopt the customs and habits of those one mingles with, to put them at their ease, is it not?"

Baumgärtner tilted his head. "Quite," he said. "You are a commoner, Miss Davies?"

"My mother is a princess," she pointed out.

"Your father is a bastard."

"He is the unacknowledged son of Baron Monroe," Tor said. "Perhaps we should sit?"

Annalies unbuttoned her coat and put it on the chair that Tor was indicating. "Not right now, thank you." She was looking at Baumgärtner.

Baumgärtner was forced to remain standing—as were they all—because the highest ranked person in the room refused to sit. He cleared his throat. "The mother of your husband, your Highness?"

"A Welsh woman of common ancestry," Annalies replied.

"I heard she was an actress," Baumgärtner said.

"An opera singer," Annalies replied. "She gave royal command performances many times. That is how Rhys' father met her—at Kensington Palace."

Baumgärtner's brow lifted. "That is not public knowledge, is it?"

"No," Annalies replied coolly.

Bronwen removed her cape as heat prickled its way up her neck. Indirectly, they were doing exactly what her mother had warned her they would do. They were turning her antecedents inside out, examining the minutiae and inspecting her teeth.

The discussion went on, as Baumgärtner and her mother tore apart her family tree, including grandparents on both sides and Annalies' own branch of the royal family.

"Is it true that your father and your uncle both suffered the family madness?" Baumgärtner asked her.

Annalies hesitated for the first time. "Your sources of information are excellent, Baumgärtner. I must congratulate you on your thoroughness. Yes, it is true. The madness was inherited."

Baumgärtner's gaze flickered toward Bronwen.

"It manifests only in males, Baumgärtner," Annalies said, with a touch of impatience. "Besides, Edvard's grandfather was as mad as March bees. He would ride his prize stallion naked through Silkeborg, waving his cutlass and calling the villagers to arm against invading Vikings."

Tor laughed, while Baumgärtner cleaned his glasses once

more and replaced them. "I see I am not the only one to have investigated."

Annalies inclined her head. "Thank you. Shall we finish this?"

Only, the discussion did not end. It continued for another hour, while Bronwen tried to ignore that it was her future they were determining. Her gaze met Tor's. He was studying her from across the room, while Annalies and Baumgärtner argued between them. His smile was small—the little one that lifted the corner of his mouth.

Her heart hurt. For a small moment, it felt as it had back in the library at Northallerton. Tor was just Tor Besogende and she had been simple Bronwen Davies. None of this silly formality had got in the way. She had been free to touch him, to speak as she wished.

Only, she had chosen to give that up, she reminded herself, in order to win Tor back...the real Tor this time, not the man who wished he was anything other than the Archeduke of Silkeborg.

Tor's smile faded. "Enough," he said.

"Your Highness?" Baumgärtner replied.

Tor shook his head. "I said, no more. This is getting us nowhere."

Baumgärtner blinked behind his spectacles. "Your Highness, these things must be examined—"

"You've done more than enough of that already, both of you," Tor said.

Annalies smiled.

Tor looked at Bronwen. "Tell Baumgärtner what you

told me, about the water and the mill. All of it."

Bronwen cleared her throat. "The paper mill is putting something into the water—most likely chlorine. That is what is making people sick in Silkeborg."

Baumgärtner snatched off his glasses. "Impossible! We vetted the mill and the operations when it was constructed!"

"Then someone is lying to you," Annalies said shortly.

Baumgärtner gasped.

"I witnessed my daughter's investigation and I trust her conclusions," Annalies added. "Hear her out."

Baumgärtner opened his mouth to speak.

"Aldous," Tor said and shook his head.

Baumgärtner closed his mouth again and looked at Bronwen expectantly.

A report was nothing more than a written essay spoken aloud, Bronwen reminded herself. She recalled the facts as she had uncovered them and explained to Baumgärtner what she had seen, what she had learned and the conclusions she had drawn.

When she was done, Baumgärtner leaned his knuckles upon the table next to him. He looked at Annalies. "Please forgive me, your Highness. I am an old man and this is... profound news. May I have your permission to sit?"

"Please do," Annalies told him. She picked up her coat and handed it to Tor, then settled on the chair, as Baumgärtner fell onto the bench behind the little table. He was trembling. This time, he withdrew a big, white handkerchief from his pocket and cleaned his glasses with care. He replaced them and looked at Tor.

"The Council will be beside themselves when they learn this."

Tor nodded. "We must investigate and establish the truth. If Bronwen's conclusions are correct then the misery of the last decade will have been resolved. That alone is cause for celebration."

"Indeed." Baumgärtner pursed his lips. "As to the other matter…" He sat up, looking at Annalies.

"No more, Baumgärtner," Tor said sharply. "I did not bring you here to find a way to object to the match no matter what. I am sure that if you were presented with the most impeccable antecedents and bloodlines possible, you would still find fault with them."

Baumgärtner hesitated. "You know the Council will be more thorough than I could ever be. You must have their agreement to move forward."

"No, I must have *your* agreement," Tor replied. "Your influence is all I need to move the Council to approve and you know it. This is the last great task you left for yourself after my father died, Aldous. Now you can see it through." Tor looked at Bronwen. His expression warmed. "I love her and I don't care who her great grandparents may have slighted, a hundred years ago. It is immaterial. I know who Bronwen really is. I got to know her in Yorkshire and you have just sampled the true woman beneath the velvet, Aldous. She has done a great service for Silkeborg. Do you not believe she will continue to serve our people, given the chance? That is the woman I want to marry and make my duchess and I want you to find a way to make it so."

Bronwen let out a breath that shook. Her heart would not stop throwing itself against her chest. It hurt. She didn't care.

Baumgärtner removed his spectacles and rubbed the bridge of his nose as if he was tired. "Then, your Highness, you'd better marry the lady."

Tor looked at Bronwen's mother. "Your Highness?"

She folded her hands on her knee. "You had better call me Annalies."

Tor smiled. "Thank you. Now, if you will excuse me?" He stepped past both of them and picked up Bronwen's hand. "Will you come with me?"

She nodded.

* * * * *

There was a widow's walk at the top of the inn. There, the air was cold, but dry and the sun was dazzling. It warmed them as Tor moved along the walk, her hand in his. He stopped and looked out over the parapet and gave a great heaving sigh.

All of Brussels lay below them, looking small and fragile. The streets were gray with snow. The sky, though, was pale blue and clear.

Tor turned to her. "I was warned by the Council and by Baumgärtner, a long time ago, that whoever I chose to marry, I should warn them of the...drawbacks of my life and give them a chance to recant. Only, I don't have to do that with you, do I?"

Bronwen held her hands together to hide their trembling. "You don't have to warn me, no. You *do* have to ask me, though, so I have something to recant."

He laughed. "I knew…as soon as I saw you last night, I *knew*." He picked up her hand and drew her toward him. "The witch was gone and a woman the world would accept as mine took her place." He brought his arm around her, holding her closer still. "You have already said yes, to everything. All of me. All of…this." He waved his free hand. "The politics, the endless bureaucracy."

"I will still need time to adjust to it," Bronwen said. "That interview just then… It was harrowing, to listen to myself being discussed in third person, with my familial flaws poked and examined."

Tor nodded. "I'm sorry about that. I had to let Baumgärtner run out of objections first, before I could make him consider you as a political asset and not just a duchess."

Bronwen laughed. "I think that might be the nicest compliment anyone has ever given me. A political asset! I will be *useful*."

Tor laughed, too. Then he let her go and got down on one knee. His thick, heavy hair fell forward over his blue eyes. "Miss Davies, would you do me the honor of becoming my wife, my duchess and the savior of my people?"

Bronwen nodded. "Yes," she whispered. "To all of it."

Tor stood and kissed her and for a moment it felt as though they were back in Yorkshire. Bronwen clung to him, breathless and tingling.

He held her face, his hands warm, despite the lack of gloves. "I love you."

"I know."

"Pretend you didn't hear me tell Baumgärtner first," he said. "Pretend I am telling you for the first time, for this is the true moment. I love you with a strength that scares me. You have no idea what my first night away from Northallerton was like. You did not see me walk the boards and scream at Baumgärtner. I went a little mad. That was when I knew I had made a mistake about you."

Bronwen put her fingertips against his lips. "No, shh…"

He kissed her fingers and pulled her hand away. "There is no reason to keep me silent anymore. I am yours and always will be."

Bronwen rested her hand on his chest, instead. "You should know I love you."

"I do." He brushed her hair. "I knew that, too, when I saw you last night. You've made a choice to be with me. You've chosen to give up that freedom you had found for yourself, for *me*. I think my heart actually stopped when I saw you in the ballroom, because I knew exactly what it meant."

He kissed her gently. On the building next to them, a clock chimed and he groaned and rested his head against hers. "It is eleven o'clock," he breathed. "The train to Denmark leaves in two hours." He closed his eyes. "If we were just Tor Besogende and Bronwen the Witch, we could run away and elope and be together from now on. Only, the people of Silkeborg would be disappointed if we hand them a *fait accompli* of that magnitude. I'm afraid I must marry you with all the pomp and circumstance the duchy can muster and that will take time to arrange. Do you mind?"

"If you can stand it, I can," Bronwen told him. "Only, can you be just Tor Besogende, for one more moment?"

His expression grew heated and he drew her to him again. "I thank God for the impulse that drove me to escape Scotland that day," he murmured, his lips against hers. "Besogende will never truly disappear for you brought him to life and gave him a reason to exist."

1866 Great Family Gathering

Anna handed Rhys the snifter and settled on the upright chair next to his armchair, as Natasha and Raymond came up to them. Raymond carried two dining chairs in one hand and held Natasha's hand with the other and was not overtaxed.

Anna turned to see if Rhys had noticed and resented the display of masculine strength, which was beyond him these days.

Natasha thanked Raymond and settled on the chair he placed next to Anna. Raymond sat on the other and crossed his legs.

"You're looking much better now, Rhys," Natasha told him.

Rhys scrubbed at his hair. "You wouldn't say that if you'd seen me after we arrived back from Denmark in the summer." He laughed self-consciously.

"That foggy London air isn't doing you any good at all," Raymond told him.

Anna kept her lips together. She had been saying for months now that the city was not conducive to good health. Rhys, though, was still a stubborn man.

Rhys sighed. "I should move to the country, yes? Grow old and moldy in a cottage by the sea?"

Raymond cleared his throat. "That would be a useless suggestion, wouldn't it? Work is all you know how to do.

Although Natasha and I did have an idea."

"You and Anna should come and live with us," Natasha said. "At Marblethorpe."

"And that isn't living in the country?" Rhys asked, his tone dry.

Anna held her silence once more.

"Not just to live," Raymond said. "There is a law practice in the village that badly needs guidance. I'm not talking about a full partnership. You could help out from time to time. Teach them what you know. It would be criminal to not pass on your knowledge, Rhys. You're one of the best barristers and solicitors in the country."

"Teaching…" Rhys breathed, staring at Raymond. No, staring *through* him.

Natasha rested her hand on Anna's knee. "Alice should come with you. Catrin, too, of course. Alice would love Marblethorpe. Brighton is barely an hour away and look what a day of sea air has done for her, already."

Anna's chest tightened and her eyes stung as she looked through the big windows at the croquet court. Alice was sitting, for she rarely had the energy to stand for long. She had defied Mortenson's calendar and was still with them. She was laughing and clapping as the game proceeded.

Rhys caught Anna's hand in his. "She looks happy," he breathed. "If Marblethorpe can make her look that way, then…"

Anna nodded. "If we do this, then there is one other condition."

Raymond raised a brow. "And that would be…?"

"I will enroll at Oxford and study for my degree."

"You?" Natasha said, startled.

"Yes, me," Annalies declared. "If Rhys and Alice are well situated, as they will be with you, then I can study during the week and return to Marblethorpe in between. It is only four years. Four years pass quickly these days."

"Annalies, you are a woman," Raymond said, his tone neutral. "Oxford doesn't allow women students. Cambridge will have Girton College—"

"Oxford needs to change its mind," Anna said. "I have the influence to force my way in there, if the rest of the family stands behind me."

"She has a point," Rhys said. "Between us, we know everyone of interest in Britain."

"Anna, you are not young anymore. You won't be able to make use of a degree, even if they grant you one," Natasha said doubtfully.

"I won't be doing it just for me," Anna replied. "I will be doing it for Sadie, who always wanted to and was denied. I'll be doing it for Bronwen, who might have chosen that life for herself if she hadn't met Tor. I will be doing it for the women who come after me, who should be given the opportunity."

Natasha smiled. "I do believe you have the capacity to do just as you say. Very well then. Rhys?"

Rhys squeezed Anna's hand. "This is what you want, my love? Why didn't you say?"

"Because you weren't ready to hear it, until now." Anna smiled at him. "It's time, Rhys."

He nodded. "Yes, it is."

* * * * *

When the knock sounded on the carriage house door, Jack jumped. No one knew he was here. He had crept away from the noise and the busy-ness for a moment. The carriage house was dusty and unused and a perfect hiding spot, only he had forgotten the memories he had made here.

He had been sitting on the stool, staring at the bed and naked mattress, when the knock came.

Cautiously, he opened the door.

Cian held up two glasses and a decanter by its neck.

Jack let the door go and moved back inside. Cian followed him.

"I thought you might call this year's Gathering off," Jack told him as he dropped the glasses on the dresser and uncorked the decanter. "You've been hiding away down here all year."

"Everyone likes the Gathers too much to cancel it," Cian said, in his deep voice. "I'm finding it…energizing, which surprises the Dickens out of me." He picked up one of the glasses and held it out.

Jack took it.

Cian held up his own glass. "I came to say thank you. For last December. For your help." He settled his hips on the dresser.

Jack took the stool. "Is that all?"

Cian tossed the brandy back in one swallow. He hissed

and reached for the decanter once more. "Also, to apologize."

Jack nodded and peered at the golden liquid. "I'm not the only one to whom you need to apologize."

"I've already caught up with Will." He lifted his refilled glass. "Will you drink with me?"

Jack sighed and touched his glass. "Cheers." He drank and raised his brows. It was the very good stock, from the back cellar, that Cian rarely allowed to be poured. "Now, this *is* an apology," he admitted and held the glass out.

Cian filled it, then looked around the room. "Every year, I try to remember to have this place cleaned out. It tends to get used, anyway." His gaze met Jack's.

Jack's chest tightened. "Don't clean it on my account," he said, his voice rough.

"As she isn't here, anyway."

"And she's married," Jack finished.

"Shouldn't you be, by now?"

Jack sighed. The letters from his parents were becoming more strident and demanding with every passing month. "I just can't bring myself to it. Not yet." He waved his empty glass. "Another," he demanded.

Cian filled it, topped his own and settled back to sip.

Silence filled the room. This time, there was no resentment or tension in it.

"Eleanore would have been married in May," Cian said casually.

Jack jumped. He studied Cian, looking for signs of the glassy, not-quite-present expression in his eyes he had seen outside the Agriculture Show in Islington. "I see…" Jack said.

Cian grimaced. "The family arranged a ceremony to mark her passing, instead."

Jack's heart squeezed. Cian's tone was matter-of-fact, hiding what had to be deep pain.

"Did you go to the ceremony?" Jack asked, for as far as he knew, Cian had not moved out of Cornwall all year.

Cian shrugged, swirling his brandy. "Wasn't invited," he said shortly and drank.

Jack sighed and drank, too. It was the only worthy response. He cleared his throat. "Cian?"

He looked up. His clear eyes were steady. Non-glassy.

"Are you…quite alright now? Are you back to normal?"

Cian considered the question. "I won't ever been the same again." He drank, a small sip, considering. "I won't ever marry."

Cold fingers walked up Jack's spine. "But…the titles…"

Cian shrugged. "Neil or Daniel will have to see to their continuation." His gaze met Jack's. "I couldn't bear it, marrying someone else." He looked away. "I will be alone. Always."

* * * * *

"No, no, you have to take your shoes and stockings off," Bronwen told him, as Tor stood watching the waves tumbling, the foam glowing in the moonlight.

"You mean, *bare feet?*" he demanded, speaking in a whisper.

"You can shout if you want, my darling. No one will hear you down here," she replied. "Plus, you must roll up your trousers."

"That is utterly barbaric."

"It is what Tor Besogende would do," she countered.

He stared at her, then bent to pluck at his shoes laces. "Sometimes I regret ever inventing that personage. You use it far too often to get your way."

"And you love it when I do," Bronwen chided him, reaching under her skirt and feeling about for the strings to her hoops. She tugged and the hoops dropped to the sand. She stepped out of them and looped her skirt up over her arm, baring her legs to her knees.

"Why, Duchess, I do believe you are wearing no pantalets," Tor teased her.

"All the better to wade in the sea with," she replied airily and walked down to where the waves washed the sand. The wet sand sank beneath her feet and she felt the delicious cold touch of it between her toes.

A wave rushed past her, bathing her ankles in chilly salt water. "I had forgotten how cool the sea is off Cornwall!" she cried.

Tor edged to the water, his feet bare and his trousers rolled up. "It cannot be as cold as in Denmark...oh!" He stopped in shock as the wave bathed his calves. "I take that back," he told her.

Bronwen giggled.

Slowly, as he accustomed himself to the water, he

moved level with her.

"Are you enjoying yourself this week, Tor?"

"I am," he said, after a pause to consider. "Meeting your family, getting to know them and their odd code and behavior…it has let me understand you much better." His smile was fleeting. "You are not the only one to romp about, here."

"For a protocol-driven Archeduke, you're doing quite well yourself in the romping department," she pointed out.

Tor looked at his bare legs and laughed. "Thank God no one can see us. The Council would be horrified."

"That was the point of bringing you here," Bronwen said. "Since Baumgärtner retired, you have been working far too hard. And in my family—"

"We do as we please," he finished.

"You're part of the family now," she added. "That means you can do exactly as you please. You can be Tor Besogende for the entire week, if you want. Not a single person will raise a single brow in your direction. No one outside the family will ever learn of it, either."

He picked up her hand, his expression sober. "Thank you for this, my love."

They stood in the moonlight, watching the waves, peace settling over them and a deep contentment.

Tor laughed and turned to her. "Do you remember, in Yorkshire, the side of the stable…?"

Bronwen caught her breath. "There is no stable here," she said as primly as she could.

"However, there is a very large rock and look, you wear

no hoops and no underthings." He drew her out of the water and up into the dry sand, his hands busy, his mouth branding her face and throat.

"Why, Mr. Besogende!" she chided him, as she hitched her skirt out of the way and wrapped her leg about his thigh.

His hand slid beneath. It was warm and large and made her shiver. "*There* she is. The woman I love…" he breathed and kissed her.

The next book in the

Scandalous Scions series.

Law of Attraction.

Her husband will divorce her for adultery, no matter the cost or the ruin it will deliver.

Knowing their love was doomed, Jenny accepted the the Duke of Burscough's pragmatic and loveless proposal of marriage to force Jack, Baron of Guestwick and heir to the Marquess of Laceby, to marry as his family wished.

Now Burscough is determined to divorce Jenny in an outrageously scandalous and public manner, while the newspapers paw over her secrets and speculate about her morals and values, as well as those of the family who raised her.

It is no longer simply a matter of whether Jack and Jenny can ever be happy together. Now, the great family itself is under attack. Can it survive the public disgrace?

Law of Attraction is the fifth book in the spin-off series following the historical romances of Scandalous Sirens. Scandalous Scions brings together the members of three great families, to love and play under the gaze of the Victorian era's moralistic, straight-laced society.

———

Praise for the Scandalous Scions series:

I love historical romances and this one filled all my likes, from a dashing, wonderful hero, a beautiful strong heroine, a love story to sigh over, side characters that are interesting, and funny, and move the story along.

About the Author

Tracy Cooper-Posey is a #1 Best Selling Author. She writes romantic suspense, historical, paranormal and science fiction romance. She has published over 100 novels since 1999, been nominated for five CAPAs including Favourite Author, and won the Emma Darcy Award.

She turned to indie publishing in 2011. Her indie titles have been nominated four times for Book Of The Year. Tracy won the award in 2012, and a SFR Galaxy Award in 2016 for "Most Intriguing Philosophical/Social Science Questions in Galaxybuilding" She has been a national magazine editor and for a decade she taught romance writing at MacEwan University.

She is addicted to Irish Breakfast tea and chocolate, sometimes taken together. In her spare time she enjoys history, Sherlock Holmes, science fiction and ignoring her treadmill. An Australian Canadian, she lives in Edmonton, Canada with her husband, a former professional wrestler, where she moved in 1996 after meeting him on-line.

Other books by

Tracy Cooper-Posey

For reviews, excerpts, and more about each title, visit Tracy's site and click on the cover you are interested in: http://tracycooperposey.com/books-by-thumbnail/

* = *Free! (in ebook format)*

Scandalous Scions
(Historical Romance Series – Spin off)
Rose of Ebony*
Soul of Sin
Valor of Love
Marriage of Lies
Scandalous Scions One
Mask of Nobility
Law of Attraction
Veil of Honor
Season of Denial
Scandalous Scions Two
Rules of Engagement
Degree of Solitude
Ashes of Pride

Once and Future Hearts
(Ancient Historical Romance — Arthurian)
Born of No Man
Dragon Kin
Pendragon Rises
War Duke of Britain
High King of Britain
Battle of Mount Badon
Abduction of Guenivere
Downfall of Cornwall

Vengeance of Arthur
Grace of Lancelot
The Grail and Glory
Camlann

Kiss Across Time Series
(Paranormal Time Travel)
Kiss Across Time*
Kiss Across Swords
Time Kissed Moments
Kiss Across Chains
Kiss Across Time Box One
Kiss Across Deserts
Kiss Across Kingdoms
Time and Tyra Again
Kiss Across Seas
Kiss Across Time Box Two
Kiss Across Worlds
Time and Remembrance
Kiss Across Tomorrow
More Time Kissed Moments

Project Kobra
(Romantic Spy Thrillers)
Hunting The Kobra
Inside Man

Vistaria Has Fallen
Vistaria Has Fallen*
Prisoner of War
Hostage Crisis
Freedom Fighters
Casualties of War
V-Day

Romantic Thrillers Series
Fatal Wild Child
Dead Again
Dead Double
Terror Stash
Thrilling Affair (Boxed Set)

Scandalous Sirens
(Historical Romance Series)
Forbidden*
Dangerous Beauty
Perilous Princess

Go-get-'em Women
(Short Romantic Suspense Series)
The Royal Talisman
Delly's Last Night
Vivian's Return
Ningaloo Nights

Blood Knot Series
(Urban Fantasy Paranormal Series)
Blood Knot
Amor Meus
Blood Stone
Blood Unleashed
Blood Drive
Blood Revealed
Blood Ascendant

The Sherlock Holmes Series
(Romantic Suspense/Mystery)
Chronicles of the Lost Years
The Case of the Reluctant Agent
Sherlock Boxed In

Beloved Bloody Time Series
(Paranormal Futuristic Time Travel)
Bannockburn Binding*
Wait
Byzantine Heartbreak
Viennese Agreement
Romani Armada
Spartan Resistance
Celtic Crossing
Beloved Bloody Time Series Boxed Set

The Kine Prophecies
(Epic Norse Fantasy Romance)
The Branded Rose Prophecy

The Stonebrood Saga
(Gargoyle Paranormal Series)
Carson's Night
Beauty's Beasts
Harvest of Holidays
Unbearable
Sabrina's Clan
Pay The Ferryman
Hearts of Stone (Boxed Set)

Destiny's Trinities
(Urban Fantasy Romance Series)
Beth's Acceptance
Mia's Return
Sera's Gift
The First Trinity
Cora's Secret
Zoe's Blockade
Octavia's War
The Second Trinity
Terra's Victory
Destiny's Trinities (Boxed Set)

Interspace Origins
(Science Fiction Romance Series)
Faring Soul
Varkan Rise
Cat and Company
Interspace Origins (Boxed Set)

Short Paranormals
Solstice Surrender
Eva's Last Dance
Three Taps, Then….
The Well of Rnomath

Jewels of Tomorrow
(Historical Romantic Suspense)
Diana By The Moon
Heart of Vengeance

The Endurance
(Science Fiction Romance Series)
5,001
Greyson's Doom
Yesterday's Legacy
Promissory Note
Quiver and Crave
Xenogenesis
Junkyard Heroes
Evangeliya
Skinwalker's Bane

Contemporary Romances
Lucifer's Lover
An Inconvenient Lover
The Contemporary Romance Collection (Boxed Set)

The Indigo Reports
(Space Opera)
Flying Blind
New Star Rising
But Now I See
Suns Eclipsed
Worlds Beyond

Non-Fiction Titles

Reading Order
(Non-Fiction, Reference)
Reading Order Perpetual*

Made in the
USA
Middletown, DE